Jos

Joseph

By John MacKenna

NEW ISLAND

JOSEPH
First published in 2014
by
New Island Books,
16 Priory Hall Office Park,
Stillorgan,
County Dublin,
Republic of Ireland.

www.newisland.ie

PRINT ISBN: 978-1-84840-383-3
EPUB ISBN: 978-1-84840-384-0
MOBI ISBN: 978-1-84840-385-7

British Library Cataloguing Data.
A CIP catalogue record for this book is available from the British Library.

Typeset by JVR Creative India
Cover design by New Island
Printed by Bell & Bain Ltd.

New Island received financial assistance from The Arts Council (*An Chomhairle
Ealaíon*), 70 Merrion Square, Dublin 2, Ireland.

10 9 8 7 6 5 4 3 2 1

For John Macdougald and Leonard Cohen,
who have kept me afloat
— body and soul, respectively —
for the past four decades.

About the Author

John MacKenna is the author of sixteen books – novels, short-story collections, memoir, poetry and biography – and a number of radio and stage plays. He is a winner of *The Irish Times*, Hennessy and Cecil Day Lewis Awards. He is also a winner of a Jacob's Radio Award for his documentary series on Leonard Cohen and a Worldplay Silver Medal (New York) for his radio play *The Woman at the Window* (RTÉ Radio 1). He lives in Co. Carlow and teaches creative writing at NUIM.

Prologue

*I*f you asked me how often I think of Ammar, I'd say very seldom, and yet, if I'm to be honest, there probably isn't a week when one or other of the things he said to me or the bits and pieces of advice he gave to me doesn't pop into my head. Funny thing, that. I must give him a call sometime or get in the van and drive up to see him. Maybe I'll do it this coming summer, when the days get longer and my head is a little clearer.

This is not how I intended the story to begin, but things have happened in the last few days that sent me on a different course from the one on which I'd set myself. I like to know where I'm going, and I like to have an idea about how I'm going to get there. I'd put that down to my trade and to the influence of Ammar. He used to say: 'If you don't know where you are, how can you know where you're going?'

Anyway, to tell this part of the story I need to take you back, long before I'd even seen or heard of Ammar, back to when I was in that strange place between the dream of manhood and manhood itself. In my experience, something almost always comes along at that point to push us over the line from the dream into the reality. Until this week, if you'd asked me, I would have said that in my case the push was my father's death. Now I'm not so sure.

My father was a good man. I think most fathers are good men, doing their best, trying to get from pillar to post, not always succeeding, but giving life their finest shot. I think of it this way. You buy twenty planks of wood and you set to work making a floor for a room. You've picked the best wood you can find, you've thrown your eye over each board, discarded what you think isn't up to scratch. And you get to work, putting the floor in place, and you do a good job, the best job you're able to do, and then the owner of the house comes along and isn't happy with the grain in one board or another. But the board is doing its job, it's solid, it's level. It may have a kink or a knot say, something that catches the owner's eye, something he or she doesn't like, but it's still doing what it was put there to do. And you try to explain this to the person who owns the house.

'It's a good piece of timber,' you say. 'It's solid and it won't warp. It'll be there long after all of us are gone.'

And you point out that no two boards in the floor are the same, that each has a peculiarity. But the owner is still not happy, and he never will be. And then someone else in the house comes along and says: 'It'll do; after a week you won't even notice it.' And someone else again in the house thinks it's wonderful, the finest piece of wood they've seen in years.

That's the best way I can describe most fathers: not all the same but doing what they are meant to do and never satisfying everyone.

If the young fellow were here, he'd have a better way of putting it. He was a great one for the stories, for coming up with little bits of tales that would make the whole thing clear, but wherever he got that talent, it wasn't from me.

My own father was a builder of sorts. He never qualified, never did his apprenticeship. That's why he was anxious for me to do mine. He set great store by qualifications. When my older brother finished his training as an electrician, my father took me aside and told me my brother was set for life.

'He has a trade, a qualification; that makes the difference. That means he can walk in anywhere and people know he's the real deal. He'll never be out of work.'

And when my brother came home in a second-hand car the following summer, a Chevrolet, my father shrugged, looked at me and said: 'Now you see what I mean?'

I loved that car. My brother had bought it from a soldier in the American base across the border. It had wide, deep leather seats, and four of us would cram into the front – my brother, my father, my mother and myself – because no one wanted to be the back-seat passenger. Sometimes my brother let me steer when we were out on the desert road, and my mother would grip my father's arm and close her eyes and we'd all laugh. And when my parents weren't about, he'd let me drive. I was 15 when he bought that car and he was 21.

I was 18, almost 19, when my father shot himself. It was the spring of 1972. No one knows why he did it. My mother never spoke about it, never offered a reason or an explanation, and my brother said he had no ideas either, but in the beginning I didn't believe him.

'I know you have, I know that you know something you're not telling me,' I said.

It was the weekend after our father's burial. I was home on compassionate leave from the Technical College. My brother said nothing.

'I don't want to be the only one who doesn't know.'

'We'll drive,' he said.

We went out through the kitchen. My mother was there, sitting at the table with three or four of the women from our street. The table was a mess of teacups and coffee cups and bread and salads and desserts. It seemed to have been like that since I'd come home. And there were two women at the sink, as there always seemed to be, and my mother was at the head of the table, talking, talking, always talking but never saying anything of consequence.

Outside, when we were in the yard, my brother tossed me the keys.

'You drive,' he said.

'What if the police see me?' I didn't have a licence.

'Fuck them. They're not going to arrest you the week after your father's funeral.'

So I drove, out into the desert.

'Drive faster,' my brother said.

I drove faster than I've ever done in my life, so fast that I terrified myself. The car windows were open and the air was rushing past. I was shaking like a frightened girl on a carnival wheel, but every time I lifted my foot from the accelerator my brother pushed my knee back down again.

'I have no fucking clue why he did it!' My brother was shouting above the scream of the wind. 'If he had a reason, then he blew it clean out of his head with the shotgun. There was nothing much left, Joe. Not a fucking thing. Just bits of hair and bone and the side of his jaw and one eye.

The rest of it was gone. Blown away. So I don't have an answer for you, and if the old lady has one she isn't saying.'

I slowed the car and brought it to a standstill on the apron of the desert. We got out and climbed onto the roof. My brother drank a bottle of beer.

'Maybe he was just fucking nuts, simple as that. Maybe he was out of his fucking head. Maybe that's the all of it, nothing deeper, nothing more profound, just madness,' my brother said after a long time. 'Madness. Stone fucking madness, too many years of wood preservative and lime and bricklaying and trench-digging and back pain and bullshit from bosses and dreams that never happened. Maybe he realised that you can't live your life through your kids and their qualifications.'

And then he threw his beer bottle out into the sand and started laughing, and his laugh was so raucous, so sharp, so inhuman that at first I thought he'd gone mad himself, but then the laughter turned to something like crying, only uglier, something that made him struggle to breathe, something frightening. I wanted to lean across, put my arm around him or touch him or something, but he was my older brother and I couldn't. Five minutes must have passed before he could speak, and when he did all the laughter and madness were gone and his voice was low and calm and slow.

'I knew him by his jaw, by the scar down the side of his jaw, the one from that car crash years ago. His eye was just a muck of tissue. I wouldn't have recognised it.'

'I'm sorry you had to be the one.'

'It's okay. Not something I'd want you or the old lady to have to do. I'll be okay. The funny thing is that his not having a face was better. How do I explain this? It was like it wasn't really him, just someone or something. Does that make sense?'

'Kind of.'

'It made it easier for me. If his two eyes had been staring back at me that would have been a lot harder.'

'I suppose.'

We sat there, looking out across the desert, watching the sun being sucked into the quicksand.

'Do you dream about him?' I asked.

My brother shook his head.

'Me neither.'

'That's good.'

'Yes.'

'That's the thing, if there had been eyes and a nose and a mouth, features you recognise about someone, you know, then I think it would have been a lot more difficult. I'm sure I'd have had nightmares then.'

The silence of the desert just sat there, like something invisible that you can't quite trust.

'It's hard to believe we're talking about our father's face, as though that's all there is of him to talk about, as though his whole life came to nothing more than a shattered jawbone and a blinded eye.'

I nodded. And then, as though the pendulum of the world had tipped, the sun disappeared.

'Now that's fucking ironic,' my brother said.

'What?'

He pointed over my shoulder and I turned. A full, fat-faced moon grinned down from an empty sky, and suddenly we were both laughing, not from anger or loss, just in relief at the contrariness of the world.

It was only when I got back to the technical college that the full impact of my father's death hit me. I knew, sitting on the bus, leaving the curled-up little village that was home — the village that, seen from a distance, is like a dried bloodstain on the desert — that I was going to lie to my friends and classmates. And I prepared myself. A work accident, a fall, head injuries. I had it all off. But what I hadn't prepared for was the dreadful emptiness that followed me onto that bus and stayed with me every mile of the way and climbed off it with me at the other end of the journey. How strange to miss someone I had hardly even spoken to in term time. My father had never answered the phone when I rang home, and if he was there and my mother asked if he wanted to talk to me I'd hear him say: 'Tell him I said hello and to keep his head in the books.' But now I missed that possibility. Something I had never done became an absence of enormous proportions, a conversation that would never have taken place became a missed opportunity, and it almost broke my heart.

Mostly I disguised the pain. I worked hard. I set myself to do even better than my father would have hoped. My aim was to be first in my class that year. I went to the college library every night, stayed till closing time. I had my projects in ahead of schedule.

It was in the library that I met Ruth. She was there most nights, and sometimes we'd nod at the bus stop, and then one night, when she was popping out of the library to get a coffee, she asked if I'd like one, and that was how things really began I suppose. She was studying languages and wanted to be a translator, to travel and know the world, as she put it. We were weeks from our exams, and I wasn't happy that the college library was closed at weekends.

'Where do you study?' she asked.

'In my house, but there are six of us and I can't say it's the quietest place. Three of the other guys have already given up on passing, so it's mayhem a lot of the time; they're just making the best of their last days here. How about you – what do you do?'

'My place is quiet. You can come over if you want.'

And so I did. She had a small flat at the other end of the town, and I'd go over at weekends. We'd study, we'd cook, sometimes we'd watch television. Once, I stayed over and we slept together, fully dressed, and only in the sense that we shared a bed. Nothing happened, mostly, I think, because I was terrified. That's when I told her the truth about my father's death.

'So sad, so sad,' she said, and she put her arms around me and kissed me and held me close to her. She put my head on her breast and I could smell the musk of her perfume. I wanted to kiss her and touch her, but I was still terrified.

The closer our end-of-year exams drew, the more inseparable we became, as though each relied on the other for support and, more importantly, for belief. My own exams ended five days before Ruth's last paper and, though I'd never done it before, I lied to my mother when I rang. I told her I wouldn't be finished till the end of the week, that one of my exams had been put back to the Friday, and that I'd need a day or two to get things tidied up.

'The cleaner and neater I leave things, the easier it'll be to get good accommodation next year,' I said.

'Yes, of course, that makes sense. You do it the right way; it's the only way.'

The naiveté of her remark made me feel even guiltier. I knew my brother wouldn't be home for another three weeks, and I knew my mother found the house lonely without my father, but I didn't want to leave until Ruth had finished her exams and we'd had a weekend together before the summer break.

And so it was. Ruth sat her final paper on the Friday morning, and that evening we went for a celebratory meal and sat up all night talking about life and aspirations and college and family, about the things you think are everything when you're 18 or 19. She had applied for a scholarship to study overseas beginning the following autumn, but whether she got an offer depended on her exam results.

'I'm not sure how well the second paper went,' she told me. 'Fingers crossed. I think the rest were okay, but it could come down to that.'

'And if you don't get it?'

She shrugged. 'I'll probably have to go and brush up somewhere during the holidays and apply again next year.'

'Would you come back here?'

'Would they want me to?' she laughed.

I said nothing, just blushed.

On the Monday morning I walked her to her bus and stowed her luggage in the hold.

'I'm glad we met,' I said. Her T-shirt was a burning red, I noticed, and it clung to her breasts. Her jeans were a sea blue. She looked beautiful in the way imminent absence makes someone even more beautiful.

'Don't make it sound so conclusive,' she smiled. 'You'll come and visit me when my parents are away. And we'll write, won't we?'

I nodded.

'And I've got your phone number. You'll answer when I call? I won't end up having to explain who I am to your mother?'

'Yes, I'll answer.'

The bus driver revved the engine, and she looked up at him from where we were standing on the dusty square. He held up one finger and grinned at her.

'You've got one more minute, darlin',' he said, 'then this aircraft is homeward bound.'

'Idiot,' she said quietly. 'But I'd better get on.'

'Yes.'

She threw her arms around me and hugged me, her lips kissed my neck and her hands were spread across my back, their warmth soaking through my shirt. I could smell petunia oil from her skin and orange blossom from her hair.

'I'll write tonight,' she said, and then she ruffled my hair and climbed the steps into the shade of the bus. A moment later the driver winked at me, the door creaked closed, the engine revved again and I lost sight of Ruth in a squall of sand. When the bus reappeared it was a hundred yards down the road and the windows were a glare of light against the high, hot sun.

I travelled home that afternoon. My bus took me in the opposite direction, almost a hundred miles from the college and two hundred miles from Ruth's home town. And when my little village came into sight, my heart coiled and dried like a dead worm in the sun. Nothing about the seven sad streets excited me, and the sight of my father's grave on the hill to the left of the road down which the bus crept made it tighten even more.

For the next two weeks there was just my mother and me. I busied myself with repainting the house and doing the odds and ends that needed doing. Each job was a reminder that my father was no longer about.

But I did other things too. I took my driving test. I made time every second day to write to Ruth, but only after I'd waited to see how frequently her letters would come. I didn't want to offend her or seem overanxious. I knew she liked me, but beyond that I was certain of nothing. I knew how I felt, but that wasn't really the issue. To be close to someone and to like them doesn't mean you know them or can necessarily expect their affection or trust in return. I imagined at the time that my father's death had taught me this lesson, but I suspect I'd known it, without recognising it, for years. Perhaps I was born knowing it.

The letters did come, two or three a week, with news about her parents, about how she was taking extra morning classes in French and English, about aunts who had arrived from abroad, about a party she'd gone to with some friends from her old school. I was jealous, imagining her hooking up with some medical student or accountant, someone who worked with his head rather than his hands, someone with a life to offer. There was a long letter from the beach where she was spending a week with her cousins. Her life sounded much more exciting and glamorous than mine, but that wouldn't have been hard. The letters included the dates and times when she would ring, with friendly warnings that I'd better be at the end of the phone because she didn't want my mother thinking that she was leading her youngest, and no doubt her dearest, astray. Did she know, I wondered, how badly I wanted her to lead me astray?

My own letters were more mundane, about the things I was doing. I concocted accounts of trips to the nearest town, twenty miles away, with my friends. The truth was I didn't have any friends with whom I'd want to go that far. My two trips to the cinema, to see *Vanishing Point* and *The French Connection*, drew immediate replies from Ruth wanting to know why I hadn't told her the plots and wondering what I thought of the acting and whether I'd recommend them.

I didn't tell her about the walk I had every evening to the cemetery with my mother, and how she had taken to bringing a loaf of bread with her to scatter among the graves. It drew dozens of crows from their rookery in the trees that lined the hedges about the burial ground. At first I thought it was just a kindness to the birds, but my mother quickly put me straight on that.

'Have you never wondered why there are so many birds in the cemetery?'

'Not really.'

'And why most of them are crows?'

'Because they nest in the trees along the perimeter.'

'Birds nest everywhere, all kinds of birds,' my mother said, scattering the last of the broken bread. The crows swooped, pecked or carried, and then returned to their perches on the headstones. 'But have you ever wondered why the crows are nesting in this place?'

I shook my head.

'Because they're the birds of the dead.'

'Birds of death?'

'No, no, no, no,' my mother said quickly. 'Not of *death*: of *the dead*. These are the souls of the people buried here.'

I laughed.

'Laugh all you like,' she said, 'but it won't change the facts. Somewhere among this flock is your father's soul. Not to feed them and him would be wrong.'

'How come no one else comes up here with bread then?'

'It's not the belief in this village, Joseph. But it is the belief in the village where I grew up, and I believe it.'

I scrutinised the crows lining the headstones to our left and right, stared into their burning eyes, scanned them for one with a crooked beak or a scarred jaw, but all the faces looked the same, black and shining, cawing and complaining that the soul food had run out for that day.

One evening I left my mother scattering the broken bread and wandered to the other end of the cemetery and read the names and dates on the older stones. And there was one with the name of a classmate, a young boy I'd almost forgotten, who had died when he was 6. He'd been in my class in the village school, and had been killed when his clothes accidentally caught fire. We'd heard him screaming two streets away. My father had refused to let my brother or me go to his funeral.

'Life is dark enough; small boys don't need to be steeped in that kind of thing,' he told a neighbour, and my mother agreed.

Afterwards, I'd sneaked up to the cemetery, convinced there'd be smoke leaking from the grave. My brother had laughed when I told him of my disappointment.

Standing there, remembering my father's consideration and trying to recall some elements of the dead boy's life, I turned and looked across the lines of stones to my father's grave. The air above it was a blotting paper of crows, their wings and bodies bent into extraordinary shapes, rising and sinking, swerving and dropping, and there at the heart of that vortex was my mother, serene, composed. Unflappable, I thought, and I smiled at my own small joke, and I smiled at the thought of her concern for these lost and hungry souls and I hoped, for that moment, that she was right in her belief.

But I wrote nothing of this in my letters. Instead, I said the weather was hot and time was moving slowly.

So the weeks passed until my brother's arrival. He had finished a contract across the border and lined up a summer's work closer to home.

'You can be my beautiful assistant,' he said.

What that meant, I soon discovered, was that I was the one with the lump hammer and he was the one with the lingo. He seemed to spend most of the day talking to the people we were working for, explaining what *we* were doing and throwing a comment my way every now and then.

'Take it handy there, Joe, don't want to damage the architrave', or 'Can you hold off there till Mrs X and myself fine tune where we're going?' Always said with the forbearance of an architect dealing with a client whose opinions he must hear out before getting on with his own great plan.

'Absolutely, Mrs X, I'll ensure that Joseph works delicately with a fine chisel around the frames of the doorways. They're beautiful, no doubt about it, and when the walls are replastered you won't even know the wires are there, I assure you.'

And, as soon as the Mercedes or the Jaguar had disappeared down the avenue, he'd hand me a hammer and off we'd go again. Not that he didn't do a good job – the old man had instilled that into us from an early age – it was just that he didn't always do it in the way the client might expect or want it to be done.

The work I liked least was crawling through the hot, crumbling attics of the old houses we were rewiring. A sudden scuttling of something in a corner, a sound of claws racing up or down a rafter, an unexpected flutter of a pigeon in my face, all these terrified me.

'How's it going? Have you laid the cable?' the voice would come from the floor below.

'Getting there.'

'Tap on the ceiling; let me know where you are.'

Tap. Tap. As far ahead of me as I could reach.

And then my brother's head would appear through the attic door, the beam of his heavy-duty flashlight would drown the weak glow of my own headlight, and I'd try not to see what had scuttled or clawed in the yards ahead of me.

'A cripple would climb Everest faster. You're only meant to be reeling out cable, there's no need to tie fancy bows on it. It's not a fucking birthday present.'

And on we went through the early summer, my brother and his beautiful assistant. And the work kept coming in.

'A lot of this has to do with the old man,' my brother said one evening while we were packing our tools neatly into the boot of the Chevrolet. Everything had a place and everything was cleaned before it went in.

'How do you mean?'

'His reputation for doing a good job – that's where our work is coming from.'

Later, when we were halfway home, he said: 'He did a good job when he killed himself too. Nothing left to chance.'

'Have you worked out why?'

My brother shook his head. 'Not a fucking clue. Who knows what was going on in that brain? Who knows anything about what goes on in anyone's brain? Speaking of which, these letters that keep coming from a certain town far away?'

I laughed.

'What's her name?'

'Ruth.'

'Pretty?'

'Yes.'

'Is she in college with you?'

'Yes.'

'Why don't you invite her down?'

'I might, or I might go up and see her some weekend when her parents are away.'

'You can borrow the car, now that you're fully legit.'

'Could I?'

'Of course. After all that crawling through rat-infested roof space, you deserve it. You don't like that bit.'

I shook my head.

'Well, as the old man would say: "Get a qualification and you won't always be doing it." '

We drove in silence for a while.

'He was a good man,' my brother said. 'Maybe we didn't give him enough credit for that when he was alive ...'.

It was the first Friday in August when Ruth's parents flew away for their long weekend. My brother and I finished work early. I'd packed my bag the night before so that all I needed to do when we got home was to shower and change my clothes.

'You'll drive safely, no rushing,' my mother said.

'I will.'

'No taking chances. *Please.*' Something in the word 'please' stopped me. The unspoken sentence that lay behind it: I don't want to lose two of you in one year.

'I'll drive slowly, I promise.'

'He'd better,' my brother laughed, winking at me. 'Never mind him; my very important vehicle is precious.'

'Back Monday afternoon?' my mother asked as they walked me to the car.

'Monday night,' my brother said. 'Give him his time.'

'And do invite the young woman down. I'd love to meet her. She has beautiful handwriting.'

'I will, and I'll drive carefully, and I'll telephone when I get there. I'll be careful about everything.'

My brother sniggered, pursed his lips, widened his eyes and pulled a face.

I managed not to smile until I was in the car and driving to the end of our street, my mother still framed, still waving goodbye in the rear-view mirror.

From the moment I turned that corner, my mind was on the road ahead, the 197 miles that lay between my home and Ruth's town, between me and her. I passed the cemetery, climbing the hill out of the village. I watched the curled shavings of streets that were my native place shrink to little and then nothing in the wing mirror, and finally cresting the hill I was clear of everyone – living and dead – and my eyes and my heart were set on the road ahead.

I laughed at my own excitement and at how great an adventure I was making of this trip. I had no idea what lay ahead, no notion of what expectations Ruth had. If I were to go back over our relationship to that point, what would I find? Warmth, friendship, a night when we'd slept together, fully clothed. Meals cooked, walks, hands held, kisses, letters, occasional phone calls that often ended unceremoniously when Ruth's parents arrived home. That was it. And yet I couldn't control my excitement. She'd waited till her parents were away to invite me. She'd telephoned just the night before to check that I was coming and to say how much she looked forward to seeing me. This must mean something.

With the passing miles and towns my nervous anticipation became excitement, and then a belief that something new and wonderful lay at my journey's end, and the idea that making love to Ruth would no longer be something imagined, something longed for but only achieved in furtive dreams.

'Three and a half hours,' my brother had said. 'It won't take you more than three and a half hours. Once you get out on the open road, you can let that baby sing.'

Once I got out on the open road a few things began to dawn on me. The fact that I'd be spending three full days with Ruth meant I'd have to have things to talk about. I didn't trust myself, so I stopped the car, scrabbled through the glove compartment and found a pencil and a used envelope. As I drove, I jotted down topics I might talk about. As the miles passed the list altered; subjects were added and others were deleted. I switched the radio from a music station to a news station, listening for the details of what was happening in the world, trying to memorise who was doing what and where and why. Then I realised I'd forgotten to buy a gift, so I had to detour to collect flowers and chocolates. I tried to think of something more exciting to take, but I couldn't. After I'd bought the flowers, I realised she'd probably have to bin them before her parents got home.

On the outskirts of the town I got lost, and it was almost eight by the time I edged the car along the wide street on which she lived, under the shade of trees that had been there for at least seventy years I reckoned. Three and a half hours, my brother had said. It had taken me almost five.

'You found me,' Ruth laughed, and then she saw the Chevy parked on the street outside. 'Wow, the famous Chevrolet. You'll have to take me out in that tomorrow.'

'Of course I will.'

We went inside, and I gave her the flowers and chocolates.

'Oh, thank you,' she said, kissing me. 'Thank you. Now ... I've got some food ready. And I mean *ready*. It's a case of on your marks, get ready, steady, go, so why don't we eat first and then I'll run you a bath and you can relax and wash away the dust of the road.'

I was in the bath when I heard her playing the piano downstairs. From nowhere, as though the music had carried the sentiment, I was over-whelmed by a sense that this relationship would never work. It was like a kind of dread flooding over me, but nothing like the terror I'd felt that night we'd shared a bed in her flat. This sensation was deeper and darker, and it washed me as profoundly as the warm water in which I was lying. It worked its way through the pores of my skin. At that time, I had nothing with which to compare it.

If you ask me now, I'll say it's like the phone ringing at four o'clock in the morning, swamping your body and your mind with dread, with the knowledge that whatever you're about to hear, it can only be calamitous.

When I look back, with fifty-nine years of my life behind me, I can identify exactly all the dark places from which that feeling materialised. It oozed from an inferiority complex instilled in me by my own inad-equacies. What had been possible in college seemed suddenly beyond me. Ruth's accent, the fact that she had grown up in a sophisticated town, the size and location of her parents' house, the fact that her father was a for-eigner – all these things conspired to make me feel that she was beyond me. The truth is that her accent had nothing to do with her personality, a town is a town, the house was comfortable but modest, her father was a man who'd had to leave his own country in search of work. But on that summer evening, it was her piano playing, the soft, beautiful notes gliding through the warm, dusky air that reminded me of who and what I was, the son of an unskilled suicide and a superstitious woman who fed bread to crows because she believed one of them to be the reincarnation of her dead husband.

So I lay in the bath with the water cooling about me and the candles Ruth had lit flickering around me. And then the piano was silent and I heard her footsteps on the stairs.

'You okay?' she called.

'Yes, sorry, I must have dozed off. I'm just getting out of the water now.'

'Run some hot water if you've got chilled.'

'No, it's fine, just getting out.'

'I'll make some coffee to warm you.'

And then the sound of her feet descending the stairs, her voice humming somewhere below. *Imagine.*

'Thanks,' I said, though I knew she couldn't hear me.

Downstairs, we sat in the warm kitchen and made plans for the following days. And then it was midnight, and the clock in the hall rang its final bells of the day.

'You must be tired,' Ruth said. 'I keep forgetting you have a day's work behind you.'

'More a half-day; I'm okay.'

'Still, we should turn in ... long day tomorrow.'

She gathered the coffee cups from the table and put them in the dishwasher. Then she switched off the kitchen light, took my hand and flicked the hall switch as we turned to climb the stairs. I followed, the lights dying behind us, the dread I'd felt as I listened to the piano music giving way to excitement, fear, hope, uncertainty.

She led me into her bedroom. My rucksack sat on a chair by her bed.

'I'm glad you're here,' she said quietly.

'Me too.'

'I'm just going to have a shower.' She kissed me, then disappeared through the open doorway. I undressed to my shorts and slid between the crisp, clean sheets. Above the bed a plastic dolphin swayed gently on a string. Three posters of David Bowie stared at me from the wall at the foot of her bed. The pillows smelled fresh and cool. And then she was back, her chestnut hair falling over her bare shoulders, a bath towel wrapped loosely about her.

'Would you like to hear some music?' she asked, nodding to the stereo on the bookshelves.

'Sure.'

'Bowie?'

'Surprise, surprise,' I laughed.

'The master,' she said, placing the needle carefully on the vinyl. The opening notes of 'Changes' filled the room and Ruth slipped into bed beside me, discarding the towel as she turned. Her skin was still warm from the shower as she snuggled against me. I kissed her mouth and then her neck. Her small breasts pressed against my skin while her hand slid down my back, slipping my pants off.

'You won't need these.'

Her tongue was in my mouth, my fingers tracing the shape of her breasts, touching her nipples, feeling them harden as I did. I wanted to tell her I'd never been with anyone like this before, that I wasn't sure if what I was doing was what she wanted me to do, but I was afraid to ask, and anyway I only wanted to think about that moment and to be lost in it because it was new and exciting and, even then, I knew I'd never feel what I was feeling again. Bowie was singing 'Oh! You Pretty Things', and my face was buried in her hair, breathing in the summer heat and the musk of her shampoo.

'Get on top of me,' she whispered, as though the house were listening to her every word. I knelt above her, her eyes green and bright, her skin flushed beneath her tan. 'It's okay, it's okay to come inside me, it's safe.' I slipped my body between her thighs, but I knew, even as I did, that it was too late, that I was coming, the seed spurting across her belly and her breasts.

'I'm sorry, I'm really sorry,' I said, rolling off her.

'It's okay. There's plenty of time. We have all night, all weekend.'

'Fuck ... I'm sorry.'

'Seriously, Joe, it's all okay, everything is okay.'

We lay side by side; her hand was in my hair and she kissed my ear and my cheek. 'Eight Line Poem' had revolved into 'Life on Mars?' before I plucked up the courage to tell her.

'That was my first time.'

She smiled. 'That's okay; we all have first times.'

'I'd been thinking about it all the way up here. Nothing else on my mind all day. All week. Not that I presumed.'

She laughed out loud.

'You're funny. It would have been okay to presume. It's not a crime.'

'It is in my family.'

'Actually, it probably is in mine, too.'

And then we kissed, and Bowie sang about 'Kooks', and by the time 'Quicksand' was playing Ruth was on top of me and I was deep inside her. My lips brushed her breasts as they moved backwards and forwards, her body arched above me, her face and neck a deeper, burning shade of red, her breathing shorter, sharper, her legs tightened about me, and then it was as though she suddenly wanted the whole house and the street and the world to hear she was coming, and I relaxed and came again, deep, deep, deep inside her.

Afterwards we lay quietly, the hum of the stereo speakers filling the silence of the night.

What else do I remember about that weekend? On the Saturday we drove out into the mountains that shoulder the sea. We ate at a road-side café and we laughed a lot. We sat on the car bonnet and looked out through the gap between the mountains, at the sea and the sky that were hard to tell apart, one blue bleeding off the other. And, as if the notion of the lost horizon had drawn our thoughts away, we talked about France and how exciting it would be if Ruth got her scholarship.

'You could come and visit me,' she said. 'We could stroll down the Champs-Élysées, arm in arm.'

'That would be lovely.'

'Wouldn't it just? I'd like that.'

'Me, too,' I said, though I knew, even as I said it, that it would never happen. I could never see myself flying to Paris. In fact I couldn't see myself flying anywhere or leaving this country, even back then. It was something that didn't feature in the lives of people in my village. Sure, my brother had crossed the border to work, but he was the exception.

'Well we'll do it. It's a date.'

And then Ruth kissed me, and her kisses were hungry, and we had sex on the bonnet of the Chevy, and I knew I'd smile every time I'd see my brother washing and waxing and polishing it in the yard at home.

Coming back that evening, on the open road between the mountains and the coast, Ruth drove. She found it hard to keep the Chevy under control.

'It's too bloody big,' she laughed, a petrified laugh. 'It's like it has a mind of its own. Like a runaway horse.'

That night we cooked and sat over the meal, talking about the time ahead. I invited her to come and stay at my mother's house for a weekend or a week.

'It won't be particularly exciting. It's a small town. Not a lot to do there.'

'I don't need to be excited all the time,' she giggled. 'Just in bed.'

Later, after we'd made love, I got out of bed and put *American Pie* on the stereo.

'This track reminds me of you,' I said. Don McLean was singing 'Empty Chairs'.

'That's a sad song,' Ruth said.

'Yeah, but the bit about the chestnut hair falling all around the pillow case, that's pretty much a good description of you … here.'

Later still, after we'd made love again, we lay in the clammy darkness and talked about music. She reckoned McLean couldn't hold a candle to Bowie.

'He's a one-single man.'

'What about 'Vincent'?'

'Okay, he's a *two*-single man. Bowie's the real thing.'

We agreed to differ.

And then the conversation turned to sex. Ruth and I were lying face to face; the only light was the yellow glow from the streetlight outside her window.

'I'm sorry about last night,' I said.

'Tonight was pretty hot,' she said quietly. 'And it's not over yet.'

'Tell me about your first time.'

Instead of words, the tears came, huge, heavy spheres falling directly to the pillow, pooling on the clean linen, her eyes closing in their wake. I put my arm around her and held her to me. Deep sobs drove through her body and into mine. One after the other they came, wracking her small frame, her face wet against my skin.

After a long time the sobbing stopped and the words arrived, broken and uncertain, a story that had nothing to do with love or joy and everything to do with opportunity.

'I don't think about it too often. Why would I? Sorry, that just happened.'

'No, *I'm* sorry,' I said. 'It was none of my business.'

'It happened. I knew him. I don't think it was planned. I was 15, he was 19. I don't even know how much I blame him. Maybe he was just stupid and rough. Maybe that's all it was. It wasn't how I'd imagined it or hoped it'd be. Anyway, it's over … gone … just gone. Let's forget it. Sorry, I must be premenstrual. Now I want to hear something cheerful.'

She leapt from the bed, wiping her face with the back of her hand and standing at the table where her LPs were stacked, flicking through them quickly.

'This is it! Carole King. 'I Feel the Earth Move'.'

Before the music began, she was back in bed.

'Now, no more sad talk. Just you and me; nothing about the past or the future. We're only allowed to talk about us and tonight and making the earth move.'

Is there anything else? We spent most of that Sunday in bed.

And that's how I remember that weekend. But it's been forty years, and memory is the most unreliable of companions, so I can only offer these recollections with the proviso that you take them as the only truth I can call to mind. They're my truth. I haven't set out intentionally to mislead; that's not what I mean. And I have something here, a piece of writing that Ruth sent me a few weeks later. It adds its own small credence to what I recall. It arrived at the end of that August, a week before I went back to college, in a letter postmarked 'Paris'. By then the college exam results were out, I was about to move on to my second year, and Ruth had taken up her scholarship to study in France. In the letter – long lost – was what I took to be a poem.

> *Unexpected kindness in the darkness of the night.*
> *Scared of your reaction, afraid of mistaken conclusion.*
> *I hesitated to say what was in my mind, thinking to myself —*

what my ideal man would say.
How he would understand without a spoken word,
holding me tight, dissolving my misery.
To my surprise – you did just that.
Flood of relief,
which found its outlet in tears. You wiped them away.
And I, who thought I knew it all
never loved you more than then.
I who hate being patronised
loved the cradling – a child again with you.

I had no idea how good the poem was, but that didn't matter. It was wonderful to get it and wonderful to read. And it was good to know I'd done something right, even if it was instinctive and even if, in truth, I'd had little notion if what I was doing was right or wrong.

But a letter is a letter, and when you're 19, even with the best will in the world, life moves on. You don't forget, but you live in the here and now and you live where you are. By the following summer the letters had dried up, and our lives were going to other places and travelling at different speeds I suppose. It's strange, though, how I kept that one piece of writing for all these years. Little did I know. Little do any of us know.

Day After Day – Badfinger

*T*he thing I like best about this work is the bits in between the jobs. Don't get me wrong; it's not that I'm not good at what I do. I am. I always have been. I've always done the finest job I can. Right from the word go, I always wanted whatever I did to be the best work possible. I had this notion in my head, from when I finished my apprenticeship, that my work was the thing I'd leave behind, and that what it said is what would be said about me, and that got me settled on taking my time and giving all I had to every job.

I still take pride in what I do, and I want it to be something I can stand over and something the customer is pleased with. That's just me and how I work. But the thing about a lot of the work I do, especially in cafés and theatres and offices, is that you can't just walk in during the day when the place is busy and start knocking walls and moving lights. You have to work around what suits people. So I might come in at seven or eight at night and work through till five or six or seven in the morning. Then I pack my tools into the van and head for home. A job could be fifty or eighty or a hundred miles from home – the farther the better as far as I'm concerned. From the day when I first started my own business, I've loved getting into the van and driving to a job. And I've loved, when I finish, packing all the work stuff into the van and hitting the road for an hour or two or three. I turn on the radio and listen to the music and get lost in my own head. That's the bit I love most, driving with the radio on in a world of my own.

I don't know if you remember that Paul Simon song, 'Cars are Cars'? He had a line in that, something about if some of my homes had been more like my cars, I might not have wandered so far. I remember the first time I heard that song. I was driving and I remember thinking, you've hit the nail on the head, sunshine, you've got it in one. He must have been thinking about me when he wrote it.

Just this evening, when I was driving home from pricing a job, I had the radio on in the van and the music was playing, and then on comes Springsteen and that opening bit with the harmonica. You know the bit that goes *Waa waa waa waa waa*. The start of 'The River'. Every time I hear that I'm straight back and it's 1975 and I'm walking down the streets of this town and my life is laid out before me. I don't know if it's the bit where he talks about no wedding day smiles and no walk down the aisle, or the bit where he wonders if a dream is a lie if it doesn't come true. Whatever it is, it just takes me back.

I was 22 when I arrived in Nazareth. I'd just finished my apprenticeship and got a job on a building site in Zip City. I'm not sure if you remember '75, but if you do you'll know that if you were working on the building sites in Zip City there was no possible way you could afford to live in the place. So I got a flat out here, in what's become my little town. Seven miles from Zip City, close enough to get in and out every day, and far enough out not to be paying top dollar. And then I started looking around for someone to share the place and split the rent.

The first guy I found was a fellow who was working on the site with me. James the Block, probably the best block-layer I've ever seen. In his prime, he'd have four men working to him and they still couldn't keep up. The other guy was the Gouger, a teacher here in the town. To be honest with you, I can't remember his name now. I've chosen to wipe it from the blackboard of my memory. But I do remember other things about him.

Like the fact that James the Block and myself would be up at half five every morning to catch the bus to Zip City. We'd grab a cup of tea and be out the door and we wouldn't be back till seven or eight in the evening. The Gouger would get up at ten to nine, be in work for nine, finish at four and be home at ten past, and we might have left two mugs on the table and they'd still be there when we got home in the evening, and he'd be sitting watching television, not a tap done.

Like the fact that one weekend I went home to see my mother, and James the Block had stayed up in Zip City, chasing some young one. I got back on the Sunday afternoon, and the minute I walked into the place I got this smell. Nothing too strong, a bit like the smell you'd get if you spilled milk in the back seat of the car and didn't wash it properly. Like the smell of milk that's just about gone off. Anyway, the next morning when we got up it was still there, and I said to James the Block: 'Do you get that smell?' He stood in the kitchen, his nose twitching like a rabbit's.

'Mmm,' he said, and I took that to mean nothing. He was a heavy smoker, so he probably couldn't smell at all.

That night, when we got home, I opened the door and the stench hit me like the wheel of a digger. I went straight into the jacks to see if that's where it was coming from. I stuck my head into the bowl and took a deep breath. I flushed the toilet and put my head in again, but the smell wasn't coming from there. I remember looking under it to see if there was a leak and banging my head off the bowl and swearing with the pain. Then I got into the bath and put my nose to the plughole, but there was nothing there beyond the smell of soap and rotting hair. The only place that was free of the smell was my bedroom, but I reckoned that was because I kept my windows open all the time. It was getting in on me. Everywhere I went it was just there, hanging in the air. And all this time the Gouger was seated in State, reading his book at the table. That's when I spotted a pile of newspapers at the side of the cooker in the kitchenette. I lifted them, gingerly, because I had a sense that I wasn't going to like what I found, and how right I was. There was this pool of dried puke on the floor and the papers had just been thrown on top.

'Did you have someone here over the weekend?' I asked.

'Who? Me?' the Gouger says.

'Yes you. You're the only one who was here. I was up seeing my mother and James was in Zip City.'

He shook his head vigorously – too vigorously. And he had this pretend look of wounded pride, like he couldn't understand how I could possibly think all this could have anything to do with him.

'Did you do this?'

Again, the shaking head and the look of hurt that might have worked on his mammy, or some young one who was teaching with him, but wasn't going to work on me.

'Well, I didn't do it and James didn't do it,' I said. 'So that kind of narrows the field.'

The Gouger said nothing, but I could guess what had happened. On the Friday or Saturday night he went on the piss, and when he got back, he, or whoever was with him, puked in the kitchen of the flat, but instead of bothering to clean it up, he just threw some old newspapers on top of the puke and went off to bed. Bloody teachers!

Not that he had it all his own way. We were a match for him, at least James the Block was. My own take on him was that he was a waste of energy and space, a knot that was easier to work around than to sand down. But James liked nothing better than to bide his time and then pick the battlefield with the Gouger. James was more interested in the well-chosen ambush than the straightforward battle.

Memories of the *encounters*, as James used to call them, come back to me. There was a night when the Gouger and some of his friends were hogging the table, philosophising over a crate of beer. It happened to be reincarnation that was up for their condescending consideration that evening, and James and I could hardly cross the kitchen without slipping in the bullshit that was piling up under our feet. Taoism and Buddhism and Hinduism and a dozen other isms were flying around the room like shavings from a door. I was reading the paper and James was washing up, and one of the Gouger's smart friends was holding court about what he'd like to come back as.

'What about James?' the Gouger asks, thinking he'd have a bit of cheap fun at the Block's expense. 'We're talking about reincarnation, about coming back in another life, in another form perhaps, or as a human being but in a different body.'

'Oh, is that what it means?' James says, pretending at innocence and confusion.

'Yes. It's an interesting concept. It raises all kinds of philosophical and moral issues, about the soul and continuity and conscience and memory. It's not just the simple matter of dying and being reborn. It comes, as Wordsworth says, *trailing clouds of glory.*'

'Interesting,' James nodded. 'What's that bit about clouds of glory thingy?'

'It's from a poem by William Wordsworth:

Our birth is but a sleep and a forgetting:
The soul that rises with us, our life's Star,
Hath had elsewhere its setting,
And cometh from afar:
Not in entire forgetfulness,
And not in utter nakedness,
But trailing clouds of glory do we come.

'Ah right. That's probably a bit above my head. And the reincarnation stuff too.'

'Possibly.'

'What you were saying to the lads there, about bringing the experiences and memories and stuff from a previous life.'

'Or lives.'

'Or lives, yes, maybe more than one life.'

Yes, it's a deep subject. As I said, people oversimplify it. But, be that as it may, if you had the chance to return, a new life, a new beginning, another chance to improve yourself, what would you like to come back as?' the Gouger asked, and I could see he was trying to set James up. He wanted an answer that he could ridicule.

James thought for a few moments. 'And I might be trailing the clouds of glory or the inglory from this life? Is there such a word as "inglory"?'

'We get your meaning,' the Gouger said.

'In that case,' James said deliberately, 'I'd come back as a boomerang.' And with that he walked off, laughing.

Another night, a party had *happened* in the flat. No one had organised it, but thirty or forty people arrived with drink. Food was organised and music was played and someone managed, despite my best efforts, to scratch one entire side of my *Captain Fantastic and the Brown Dirt Cowboy* album. And it wasn't any of my friends.

Anyway, by some miracle, the Gouger shifted a young one. Another teacher, I think. I do know she was pretty pissed. She'd have to have been to go anywhere with him. They sneaked out of the living room, down this stairs at the back of the flat, a kind of upmarket fire escape that we never used. James the Block saw them going out, and the Gouger made the mistake of winking at him and saying: 'At least some of us know how to charm a woman, Block.'

James nodded and said nothing. Instead, he waited about twenty minutes, giving them time to get into a good clinch, and then he meandered out onto the stairs for a smoke, all innocence again. From what he told me, he stood on the top step, smoking away, while the pair below were going at it hammer and tongs. And then he started to sing, quietly but loudly enough to be heard, a rhyme he'd learned as a child. He claimed it just came back to him. *Long and thin goes too far in and can be rather chancy, short and thick does the trick and suits the lady's fancy.* And then he left them to it, knowing the damage was done.

The shit hit the fan the next morning, and I woke up to hear the Gouger and James going at it in the kitchen.

'How dare you do what you did?!' the Gouger was shouting.

'Do you know what – you give me too much credit,' James comes back. 'Sure I wouldn't have the brains to be that conniving. It was an honest mistake. I didn't know you were there. I just wandered out for a smoke.'

'You know damn well that's a lie. You saw us going outside. You're a devious bastard.'

'If you say so. Who am I to argue with your superior knowledge and education?'

'It was a low, mean, envious, cheap and invasive thing to do.'

'Back up, back up … you lost me there at envious.'

'You're a thick, ignorant man, Block …'.

'That's what I'm telling you,' James interrupted. 'I *am* thick. You know that and your friends know that, so how could I have the wit to plan, let alone carry out, a devious, and invasive – was it invasive you said? – manoeuvre like that?'

'Fuck off!' the Gouger shouted, and he didn't speak another word to either of us for five days.

'Peace, perfect peace,' James laughed, and he was right.

Now and again the Gouger would flare up and James would sit and listen, dragging on the eternal cigarette, blowing smoke rings, saying nothing, letting him rant, agreeing with him, knowing this enraged the Gouger even more. And sometimes, when the rant had died down, James would throw in something, just to get things going for his own entertainment.

And the barbs always began with *Do you know what?* Once I heard that phrase, I'd wait for whatever followed.

'Do you know what,' James would say. Your shit is chocolate cake; you must serve it up some night for dessert – sorry pudding' or 'Do you know what, you're as cold as the balls of a corpse.' And off they'd go.

The more I think about that time, the more things keep coming back to me. There was the evening when the Gouger brought home another young one – another teacher, naive and impressed by his bullshit. He always seemed to be torn between wanting to impress us with his latest conquest and the risk that James would feck things up for him. This time the Gouger was holding forth about masturbation and how ridiculous it was that it was frowned on in some cultures. I knew he was trying to show his liberal credentials – and a few other things – to the young woman. But James wasn't having any of it.

'Do you like music?' James enquired.

'I do,' the young woman said.

'Glen Campbell?'

'Not quite my type of music,' she said politely.

'James likes hillbilly tunes,' the Gouger sniggered.

'I do,' James said. ' "Rhinestone Cowboy" is a great song.'

'I can't say I know it,' the Gouger lied.

'You should have a listen. Do you know what, it reminds me of you,' James said, and then he began to sing in a clear, slow voice. *'Like a nine-stone cowboy, riding out in a hearse with his newfangled dildeo ...'.* 'Do you mind? We have company,' the Gouger interrupted.

'Oh, sorry, sorry,' James says, all humility. 'I thought you were talking about wanking a few minutes ago.'

'Do you have to drag everything down to the lowest level?'

'It's my natural home. Aren't you always telling me that?'

That winter the Gouger came down with a heavy cold. One of the side effects was that he temporarily developed tinnitus. One night, while the three of us were watching something on TV, the Gouger began to complain that the volume needed turning up. At this stage the volume was so high that the ashtray on top of the telly was hopping.

'If it goes any louder we'll be reported for a breach of the peace!' James shouted.

'You're not suffering with tinnitus,' the Gouger moaned.

'Have you ever considered,' James asked, 'that what you're hearing may, in fact, be an echo caused by the fact that your head is so far up your hole that your ears are meeting your words coming back down? I think the medical term is "sphincteritis", but I'm open to correction on that one – so don't quote me till I get a chance to check the medical encyclopaedia.'

The last girlfriend the Gouger ever brought to the flat was a very well-spoken, very proper young woman, a legal secretary. She was grist to James's mill.

'I'm James,' he said as he shook her hand, assuming this very la-di-dah accent. 'I'm a humble block-layer, but I'm very pleased to meet you. And this is my friend, Joseph. He's a carpenter, very good at the tongue in groove.'

At one point the conversation turned to restaurants.

'Do you like eating out?' James asked.

'Of course, of course I do,' the young woman smiled.

'Yes, me too,' James said, and he grinned a drooling, salacious grin. I could almost see the Gouger's skin begin to crawl with terror and embarrassment.

James's parting shot that night, as he headed for bed, came as an interruption to a discussion on careers and ambition.

'You know what they say,' he said quietly, leaning over the back of the couch and smiling sweetly at the young woman.

'No. What do they say?'

'If at first you don't succeed – suck harder! Goodnight, sweet lady.'

Not once in the hour had his accent dropped.

Cheap entertainment.

The other thing I remember about that flat is the flagpole out the front. Those were the days when the national flag was flying everywhere, like we had to prove to ourselves again and again that we were patriotic. This flag had a rope that slapped against the metal pole, day and night. The slightest breeze and it went *twep twep twep* all night long. Until James cut the rope.

'You could be arrested for that. That could be interpreted as an act of treason,' the Gouger said.

'Fuck them. Let them take me out and hang me with the rope; at least I'll get some sleep in the meantime.'

The rope was replaced, and cut again, and replaced again, and then, mysteriously, the flagpole was sawn at the base and left lying in the street. It must have taken some effort to cut through the metal, and the pole was never replaced.

'It'd take someone with the right tools and the right know-how to do that,' James smiled. 'A simple-minded block-layer would never manage that.' And we all slept soundly from then on.

The First Time Ever I Saw Your Face – Roberta Flack

That was small-town life for us back then. But mostly it was hard work. James and I caught the bus in and out of Zip City every morning and evening. I don't know if you remember what this country was like back then, but the journey might take twenty minutes or it might take an hour and a half, depending on whether the army decided to stop the bus and come on board. If they did, we'd all be herded off and searched. Tool bags would be emptied and the tools scattered all over the place. The luggage compartment would be turned out and every bag and package gone through. And the same thing could as easily happen coming home.

If we arrived late, the Gouger would be there at the table, correcting homework or reading his newspaper.

'Home are the heroes,' he'd say. 'Don't tell me the army stifled the revolution. Again!'

We got into the habit of lying and saying we'd been doing overtime, but he never believed that story – even when it was true.

Sometimes in the evenings and at the weekends I'd go down to the only coffee shop in the village – Jacob's Ladder it was called. Don't ask me why it was called that, because the guy who owned it was named Esau. Probably Esau's Ladder didn't have the same ring to it. Apparently, he'd opened the coffee shop in the Spring of 1972, but it didn't take off, so he closed it that autumn and disappeared for ten days. When he got back he had this huge crate on the bed of his pick-up truck. It took him hours to clear a space and manhandle the crate inside. No one was allowed to help or even take a peep at the mystery package, and the village was agog with rumours. The coffee shop windows were covered with newspapers and the door was kept locked. Finally, the following weekend all was revealed. *Dah-dah* – the village's first jukebox, a gleaming capsule of words and music. Not only that, there were a hundred shining new singles inside, the major hits of 1972. They were all in there: 'Popcorn'; 'Lean on Me'; 'Brandy (You're a Fine Girl)'; 'Betcha by Golly, Wow'; 'Long Cool Woman in a Black Dress'; 'Back Stabbers'; 'Beautiful Sunday'; 'In the Rain'; 'Black and White' – the whole shooting gallery. The kids flocked in, and what had been a dead duck took off like a rocket.

James had this habit, when the place was full of teenagers, of putting a handful of coins in the jukebox and selecting eight or ten B-sides and letting them play through. That really pissed off the kids.

'Come on,' they'd say. 'You're hogging it with crap music.'

And James would smile and wink at them and say, 'You pays your money, you takes your chances. I'm partial to the occasional B-side.'

And the kids would say: 'Oh come on, you're just pricking around,' and then they'd appeal to Esau, but he'd shrug and flip another burger.

By the time I'd finished my apprenticeship, got the start in Zip City and found the flat here it was 1975, and Jacob's Ladder was still going strong and the jukebox was there in the corner. The problem was that it also had the same, original hundred singles in it. When you walked through the door it was like stepping back in time, musically speaking. Is retro the right word for it? Anyway, stepping into Jacob's Ladder was a trip back to 1972.

By then the chair dances had started. When James the Block told me about them I thought he was taking the piss.

'Every Monday night – *Eight till late*, that's what the poster says.'

'Give us a break,' I said. 'You're not dealing with the Gouger now.'

'Come down with me and I'll show you.'

So off we went on the following Monday evening. And the only word I can think of that can even begin to describe what I saw is 'bizarre'.

There were all these old ones and old fellows inside. They were probably younger then than I am now, but they looked like old ones and old fellows to me.

The thing about chair dancing was that you could only dance while you were sitting down. You were free to get up and walk around between the sets, but once the music began you had to be sitting at the counter or in one of the booths. Everyone lined up waiting for the music to begin, and then the record would flick onto the jukebox turntable and the old folks would start dancing. From outside, looking in, it was like watching synchronised swimming. All the old people making these choreographed moves, the New Seekers singing about how they'd like to teach the world to sing, and all these gnarled hands going up to their mouths and miming the drawing out of the song. *In perfect harmony* – arms crossed in unison on breasts. *Apple trees* – the arms go up like branches. *Honey bees* – long fingers racing like demented wings through the air. *Snow white turtle doves* – an ascension of liver-spotted hands in the air. And so it went, on and on, one song after another. I was fascinated and mystified at the same time. The whole thing was weird and mesmerising. But, after ten minutes, James was just bored and itching to be gone. I supposed it wasn't new to him.

'Come on,' he said. 'We've seen enough. It's like a lunatic asylum for the legless and footless and foolish.'

The amazing thing is that the Monday night chair dances went on until the place closed in 1998; as one of the dancers would die, their place would be taken by someone else who had come of age. There seemed to be a waiting list for people to get in, a bit like a departure lounge for the dying. And always they chair danced to the same songs from 1972.

Anyway, Jacob's Ladder was where I'd go for something to eat whenever I didn't feel like cooking. Or I'd wander down for a break at the weekends. It was the kind of place where you could go in and read the papers over a cup of coffee and Esau would never ask, 'Is there anything else you'd like?' the way they do in a lot of these places. It was just a relaxing spot, unpretentious.

I remember one Friday evening, at the end of June '75. James the Block had stayed on in Zip City for the weekend, chasing some young one whom he'd described to me in great detail in the building site.

'I'm telling you, she's the business. Unbelievable. She's a milking machine! And she goes down faster than the *Titanic*.'

I'd arrived back to the flat that evening to discover the Gouger seated at the table, and I'd taken one look at him and thought, no – I really don't want to spend the evening sitting here, trying to have a bite to eat and listening to this guy talk bullshit. So I had a shower and headed for Jacob's Ladder. I bought the paper on the way and sat in for something to eat and a nice, relaxed read.

I was there a while, at the coffee and dessert stage, minding my own business. There were six or eight schoolgirls in the corner booth. They'd finished school that afternoon, not just for the summer but for good. They were celebrating, drinking Pepsis and coffees and laughing and having a good time. But they were noisy, really noisy, and I was finding it hard to concentrate on what I was reading. So I got up to put on some music, something loud to drown them out. I walked over to the jukebox, slipped my coins in, and I was standing there, reading the extensive and crackly hits of '72, trying to find the loudest track available, when I sensed someone standing beside me. It was one of the girls from the corner booth.

'What are you going to play?' she says.

I shook my head, shrugged and gestured to the jukebox. Bloody nerve, I thought.

'You choose. Never mind that I pay the piper, you might as well call the tune.'

And with that I stepped away, left her to it, walked back to my seat and started reading my paper again. She spent an age making up her mind about one song. Every now and again I'd look up and she was still there, flicking through the lists. Finally, she pressed two buttons and I heard a record flop onto the turntable and then the familiar *dum dum, dum dum* of the piano, the opening notes of Nilsson's version of 'Without You'.

The next thing I know is, the girl comes over and stands beside me and asks me to dance.

'I'm not a dancer,' I said, and I was laughing; I didn't even take my eyes from my paper because I thought she was winding me up. 'I never have been and never will be.'

But she didn't walk away, and when I looked up I could see in her eyes that she was serious. I don't know if you've ever been in the position where someone has asked you to dance. If you have, you'll know that you have two choices. Either you can say 'no' and seem like a plonker, or, if you're like me, you can say 'yes' and prove that you are a complete plonker.

So I got up and we stood in the small space between the booths and the jukebox. For a moment I had no idea what to do, and I thanked the heavens that the Gouger wasn't around. But the girl took my hands and put them on her back and began to dance.

When I said I couldn't dance I was telling the truth. In our little village we had a phrase to describe people who danced like me: 'farm dancers'. Farm dancers stand in one place, they move their left leg towards their right and back again, then they move their right leg towards their left and back again and so it goes on. And on. And on. And on.

On the other hand, slow farm dancing involves shuffling the feet and following the partner's lead, and that's about it. You stay close and you keep up and you pray for the music to end.

So we went on dancing in the narrow space. To be honest, I was half-hoping Esau would step out from behind the counter and bellow, in that deep, rich voice of his: 'No dancing please, except on Monday nights.' But he didn't of course. He just got on with what he was doing.

And then I was waiting for the smart remarks to start from the other girls in the corner booth, waiting for the jeers and the comments on how bad a dancer I was. But they never came. Instead, there was silence from that corner of the coffee shop. Just the music from the jukebox and Nilsson singing that sad, sad song. And while he sang about tomorrow and thinking of your sorrow, the girl put her head against my shoulder and I got the fresh smell of apples from her hair. It wasn't apples, of course, it was apple shampoo, but the scent was beautiful. And I felt her fingers on the back of my neck, and for those few moments I began to believe that I actually could dance as well as any man alive. And then the music faded and I stood there, uncertain what to do or say, until, in my confusion, I said 'thanks,' smiled, turned and walked back to the booth where my coffee was cooling and my k'nafeh was waiting. But instead of going back to her friends she slid into the seat opposite, reached across and, taking the spoon from my coffee cup, pulled my plate of k'nafeh to her side of the table and began to eat.

And that was Miriam, and that was this town in 1975. She was 17 and I was 22, and we started going out that night. Right through the long days of summer and into the autumn we were inseparable. I'd just bought a motorbike, and we'd head off in the evenings or at weekends. Sometimes we'd spin into Zip City to see a film or we'd head out into the country and stop off at some greasy spoon to eat something totally unhealthy. We were young and fit and life would last forever and happiness was a world without end.

There were summer evenings when we'd stretch the day to the place where it breaks. Miriam would tell her parents she was going somewhere with one of her school friends, and I'd pick her up at Jacob's Ladder and we'd head for the coast or out to the open countryside, anywhere that took us away from the streets and the eyes and the whispers.

I don't think about those times too much. How can I, without feeling lost or bitter or both? But when I do allow myself that journey, like I'm doing now, there are a handful of days that draw me back, the gentler days before the hope and the promise expired. The evening we stopped at the gate of a meadow and Miriam said it looked like we were the first people ever to have walked there. The grass and the flowers were thigh-high, and we waded through them, out to an island of our own making, and we lay down there with the summer sun still high in the shining sky. The grass smelled of childhood. I remember lying with my hands behind my head and Miriam lay beside me, her arm across my chest, and the small birds were plunging through the blue and yellow air, miniature kamikaze pilots, changing their minds at the last second and shooting off again into the blinding angles of the sun. We talked and talked, though I have no idea now what it was we talked about. I find it hard to believe, never mind remember, that we could find anything to talk about at all. But I do remember the birds and the sky and the smell of the grass, and I do remember how happy I was and how strongly I believed that our lives would become one life that would last forever.

I saw a couple today; they live on the next street to this. They were walking back from the shops or somewhere, and he was wearing a warm coat and she was laughing and I know they've been together for thirty-five years or more, and they looked so happy, so at ease and so healthy in each other's company, and I envied them.

Storm in a Teacup – The Fortunes

I never picked Miriam up from her house. We'd meet at the end of her street or at Jacob's Ladder, but never at her house. Her father wasn't a nice man, and that's putting it mildly. He was one of these little fellows who wanted to be a big fellow. He'd opened a shop here years before, it sold knick-knacks, *Fancy Goods* as it said over the door, cheap and cheerful – unlike himself. Then he opened a branch in Zip City, and then another. By the time I met Miriam her father had this vast empire of three shops. He was the kind of man who needed to prove himself every day. I can't say I ever met anyone who truly liked him. I remember someone saying to me once that he was the kind of guy you wouldn't want to be with, even on his birthday, which was ironic because the first time I met him was on his birthday.

I remember the day of the party. It began as a pleasant, sunny October morning. I was working on a building site in Zip City with James the Block, and I was having second and third thoughts about the party. To be honest, I was seriously thinking of doing a runner and not turning up at all.

'You can't do that,' James says. 'You can't just not turn up and leave the girl high and dry. She'll be depending on you to be there. You're not going to do that. You'll never forgive yourself if you do. And neither will she.'

So I went. I didn't take the motorbike because I assumed her father would frown on it. Instead, I walked. Going up their street I realised just how big-league the area was. Huge houses with well-kept gardens and lots of trees everywhere, with sprinklers whirring on the lawns, greenery where there shouldn't be any. I consoled myself with the thought that there'd be a lot of people in the house and I could keep myself lost in the crowd. And that's where I got it totally wrong.

Miriam opened half of the huge, studded door that had brought down at least one fine tree. She kissed me quickly, too quickly, and then led me across a tiled hall that could have housed a five-a-side football pitch and into this massive living room where I was met with the sight of a long table laid out for dinner, but with only six settings. The crowd I was expecting turned out to be Miriam, her mother, her cousin Liz and her boyfriend, myself and Miriam's father. He was already seated in splendour at the top of the table.

No sooner had the meal begun than he wanted to know my seed, breed and generation.

'So, Joseph, where is it exactly that you call home?' Despite the empire of three shops and the big house and the silver cutlery, he hadn't learned the art of swallowing his food before he spoke, so the words came out something like, *So Wosep wheah is ih eggockly tha you cah home?* And then the interrogation went on. 'Tell me about your father's people?' 'And your mother's family?' 'And do you have brothers and sisters?' 'And your aspi-rations, work-wise? You have ambitions I presume?' 'Where do you see yourself in five years' time?'

I knew exactly what he was doing. Information is ammunition to people like him, and I was damned if I were going to give him any, so I stuffed him with as many lies as I could concoct, and by the time we'd finished the main course I was beginning to enjoy the game. I remember thinking that James the Block would have been proud of me. Miriam's father was what James would label *the two ends and the middle of a prick of the highest order*, the kind of person who glories in putting other people down because they believe that leaves them room to build themselves up. And, anyway, I could console myself with the thought that I wasn't going out with him; I was going out with his daughter.

Those were good times. I was happy. I was working. I was in love. I was loved. James and I travelled to and from work in Zip City, sometimes by bus, sometimes on my motorbike. On average we were stopped by the army three or four times a week between coming and going. It was a pain in the ass, but not as bad for us as for the guys travelling in vans. They were stopped every day, sometimes twice on the same journey. There'd be a roadblock, and they'd be ordered to take everything out of the van. Often they were made to take the wheels off, one by one, jacking the van up, removing the wheel, putting it back on and then going to the next wheel. It could take up to an hour, and then everything had to be put back in the van. The chances were that two miles down the road they'd be put through the same routine again. The trick was not to rise to any of the provocations; getting annoyed played into the soldiers' hands. They liked nothing better than a long, pointless argument, and it guaranteed you further trouble up the road. They'd become suddenly forgetful, telling you that they couldn't remember you taking off the front wheels and would *Sir* mind doing it again. The trick was to keep your mouth shut and your face expressionless.

Once I was sent out on a company lorry to collect a generator from another site, and that was a nightmare. We were stopped and made to unload the generator, and a couple of steel girders that happened to be in the trailer. What should have taken us half an hour ended up taking three and a half hours. The bigger and heavier and more awkward the cargo, the more likely we were to be ordered to unload it. But, as far as I was concerned, it was no more than a pain in the ass, something we lived with and laughed about afterwards.

'Not a patch on an evening spent answering questions from Miriam's father,' as I told James one morning when we were stuck in a checkpoint queue outside Zip City. 'Now there's a boy who could teach the army a thing or two about interrogation methods.'

Let's Stay Together – Al Green

*T*hat's how life was for Miriam and me, right through the autumn and winter and into the early part of 1975. We'd see each other a couple of times a week. Now and then I'd have to call to her house, just to keep up appearances, but mostly we met at the coffee shop and stayed there or went somewhere on the bike. We rarely went back to the flat because I didn't want the Gouger trying to make an impression by doing me down. You could say that was my own problem, you could argue that I had an inferiority complex, and you might be right, but it didn't seem to be worth the trouble. And even if James the Block was there and in top form, it just meant there'd be a sparring match between him and the Gouger, and that wasn't my idea of a good time. So Jacob's Ladder was our middle ground. We'd laugh about it.

'We're like the lost tribe,' Miriam would say. 'Can't go one place and can't go to the other.'

I bought her a copy of *Tonight's the Night* for her birthday because she loved Neil Young and she was always singing 'Come on Baby Let's Go Downtown'; it kind of became our theme song during that winter.

Then one evening, at the end of March '76, we met in Jacob's Ladder as usual. It was a Friday evening and we had got into the habit of meeting for coffee after Miriam finished work in her father's shop. I was telling her about James the Block, something he'd said or done on the building site that day. And she was telling me about some incident that had happened in the shop. An argument had broken out between two elderly women about an ornamental swan that both claimed to have seen first.

'They just went at it for ten minutes. In the end, I walked into the storeroom and brought a dozen boxes out to the shop and lined twelve identical swans up on the counter. And then, wait till you hear this, one of them turned to the other and said, cool as you like: "If they're that common, I wouldn't want one." And the other old bat says: "Neither would I. Come on." And the two of them head out the door like best buddies, all nodding heads and *tut tut tut.*'

We talked for a while about what we might do for the weekend and then, out of the blue, Miriam told me she was pregnant. I was stunned. I had no idea what was expected of me, what to say or what to do. I never know what to say in situations like that, and anyway I didn't get much of a chance to say anything because she started telling me how wonderful it was and how brilliant and how special. And I was sitting there thinking, yeah, yeah, it sure is special because I had absolutely nothing to do with it, I wasn't even in at the start of it. And then she was talking about how exciting our lives would be and about the happiness that we'd have and how this was the start of a whole new adventure and I was sitting there, still saying nothing. And the next thing I know is she's telling me how she'd been standing at her mother's kitchen table about a month before and she'd turned around to get something and the kitchen door was open, the wintry sunlight coming low through it, and there was a stranger framed in the doorway.

'The light was behind him and I couldn't see his face clearly, I couldn't see the features,' she said, and her voice was low but it had this intensity, like she was still seeing it. 'The light was just coming off him, Joe. It was blinding, and there was this aura around him, shining, like it was all ruffled light or something. And there was a heat coming from the doorway, light and heat that just broke over me like a really balmy, tender wave.'

And that was where I flipped.

'Listen,' I said. 'I don't mind you telling me you're pregnant. In fact, I'm glad that you feel you can tell me. That's a good thing. I'm really glad you felt you could. And I don't even really mind who the father is. That's between you and him. But I don't want you sitting there treating me like a total and complete gobshite, telling about this character in your mother's kitchen door, this bright, shiny character with fluttery, feathery wings or whatever he had. That's bullshit.'

I caught Esau's eye, and I could see that although he liked me and we got on really well, he liked Miriam too, and he wasn't impressed by the tone of my voice. I don't think he could hear what I was saying, but it would have been plain to see I was angry. But, if I'm honest, I didn't really care at that stage. I was furious. I sat there, my leg jigging under the café table, waiting for Miriam to say something, but she didn't have a word to say, nothing but silence.

'Just … just … just go fuck yourself,' I spat, and I picked up my jacket and stormed out.

The motorbike was parked on the street outside, so I got on it and roared out of there. I drove and drove and drove. I had no idea where I was going. I just wanted to be away from the place. And all this stuff was going through my head, all this nonsense going round and round in a jumble, like clothes in a spin dryer, caught up together. Then I'd start to separate one thing from another and then they'd get jumbled again. Part of me wanted to turn the bike around and go back and listen and talk, and part of me was just so angry that she'd done this to me.

I was driving like a lunatic, but I knew I couldn't go back to the flat because the other two guys were there. They knew I was on a date, and the Gouger would spot that I was back early and want to know why.

'Oh. Did Romeo and Juliet having a falling out? Is she sitting some-where keening? "Romeo, Romeo, wherefore art thou Romeo?" ' I could just imagine him, and there was no way I was going to give him that pleasure.

So I just kept riding till I was out in the middle of nowhere, and then I stopped the bike and parked it in a gateway and sat on the ditch at the side of the road in the pitch darkness. I must have been out there for hours.

It was well after midnight when I got back on the bike and drove home. When I got to Sycamore Street, I wheeled the bike the last 300 yards. The flat was quiet, in darkness, the other pair asleep. I got into bed, closed my eyes and didn't sleep a wink all night.

The following morning, long before it got bright, I was up. I wheeled the motorbike out into a little courtyard that was in front of the flat and started working on it by the beam from the street lamp. And all the stuff from the night before was going round in my head again, like the bloody cycle would never end. Part of me didn't believe I could live without see-ing Miriam, and part of me never wanted to see sight or light of her again.

Anyway, I was working away on the bike, and I leaned over to pick up a spanner and, as I was picking it up, I glanced down the street and the sun had just risen, the glow coming in really low and flat, and it blinded me for a minute. And then, out of the scarlet light, I saw this figure about a hundred yards away – a small, frail figure with all this brightness around it. I couldn't make out who it was, just that there was an outline of someone on the street, and then, as the figure got nearer and I shaded my eyes, I realised it was Miriam.

She looked so fragile, so thin. It was like the slightest breeze could just lift her off the face of the earth and carry her away. And part of me wished that it would, that a wind would come from the heavens and just lift her clean out of my life. And another part of me just wanted to put my arms around her and protect her and look after her. I pretended to work on the motorbike, and she came and stood beside me for a long time, her shadow stumbling over me. She stood there for what seemed like an age until, finally, I barked: 'What do you want?'

'I just want to talk,' she said, and I knew by her voice that she'd got as little sleep as I had.

I put down the spanner I was holding and we sat on the pavement and talked and talked and talked for hours, literally. We talked so much that finally I was just worn down; I was out of energy.

'Look,' I said, and I put my arm around her, 'you know I care about you.'

I knew she wanted me to say that I loved her, but in that moment I just couldn't get the words out. *Care* was the best I could muster.

'What I want for you to do is to go back home now, pack a bag and leave it somewhere that you can get it quickly, just in case, just as a standby. I'll come up at ten and we'll tell your parents. Okay?'

She nodded.

'I'll see you at ten. Now go on, go home and pack. Just in case.'

I finished my work on the bike, went in and packed a bag myself. I had a feeling I'd need it. And then, at 10 o'clock I drove up to her parents' house and parked the bike outside. Her father's car was in the drive. I knew his morning routine. It never changed. Rise early, make an inspection of the vast empire, check on stocks, put through orders, and then back home at 9.45 for breakfast.

Miriam's parents were in the kitchen, her father seated at the head of the table, stuffing himself with food. Her mother was standing at the kitchen sink. She smiled. He looked up and frowned. Ironically, the kitchen door was open onto the sunny courtyard outside, the morning sun streaming through it, painting a crooked, rectangular shape on the kitchen floor.

'Unusual to see you here so early in the morning, Joseph,' Miriam's father muttered through a mouthful of toast and scrambled egg. 'There must be a blue moon due or something.'

And then we told them. The first thing that happened was that everything was swept off the table, crockery and cutlery crashed and clanged on the tiled floor. I didn't mind that; I was expecting it. The next thing that happened was that a chair hit the wall behind my head, and I didn't mind that; I was expecting that too. Then the table was overturned, and I had to admire her father's determination. It was a fine piece of furniture, solid cedar, and it took some effort for a guy of his size to overturn it. Then her father crossed the kitchen and his face was about six inches from my chest, turned upward like a flaming sun, shooting out asteroids of egg and bread that spattered my face. But I put up with that too, and with the *'How dare you's'* and *'Do you realise what you've done's'* and *'I'm tempted to's.'* I let it all go by until he turned to Miriam and shouted: 'And you, you … you little whore.'

When I got back to the flat, I put my hand in a bucket of ice and, eventually, the pain eased and the swelling began to subside. Once that happened, I had a quick word with James and gave him a month's rent. Then Miriam and I put our bags on the back of the bike and headed for the border. I drove fast, as fast as I dared. Miriam's arms were around my waist, and I could feel the heat of her body against my back and the tightness of her small fists, locked into my stomach. And while we were riding my hand was throbbing, but I couldn't help laughing and thinking that, bad and all as my pain was, it was nothing compared to the pain and humiliation of a mouth full of broken teeth.

We kept going, not a stop for coffee or water or anything. Just drove and drove and drove. Every so often I'd shout: 'Are you okay?' and she'd shout back, 'Yeah' or 'Fine,' and I'd put my head down and step on the gas again. Flat out till we crossed the border into Egypt. Only then did we stop.

I parked the bike on the roadside and we stretched our legs. Neither of us spoke for a long time, just stood there looking back across the border, grinning and happy, shy almost. Almost afraid to kiss or hug. And then I saluted the land we'd left.

'*Adios!*' I shouted, and then Miriam shouted, too: '*Adios!*'

The Baby – The Hollies

I was blessed in Egypt. On the second or third site I went to, looking for a start, I met this guy called Ammar. He was the foreman. The minute he opened his mouth I knew exactly where he was from, and the moment I opened mine, he knew where I was from – two villages no more than twenty miles apart. Sometimes an accent is a handy thing. He gave me a start, labouring, and once he realised I wasn't afraid to work and that I actually knew a newel post from a window frame, he put me to carpentering. By the end of that summer I was in charge of that end of things.

Ammar and his wife, Rania, helped us find a place to live, and his wife took Miriam out for coffee, showed her where the markets and shops were and generally helped her to settle in.

Ammar was the guy who suggested I grow a beard.

'If you ever consider going into business on your own in this game, Joseph, consider this point,' he said, and his tone became serious and his language quite formal, and his index finger was directed somewhere over my left shoulder, as it always was when he wanted to make a point. 'If you ever consider that possibility, or if you want to pull in some extra work in the evenings or at weekends in order to support your young wife and child, grow a beard. That's my advice to you. Grow a good beard. Now this is very important, trust me. I give you the benefit of years of experience. This beard must not be too long, Joseph, or unkempt, otherwise people will think you're a hippy and they'll avoid you.'

I laughed, but I didn't contradict him on the wife bit.

'You sound like my father, telling me the facts of life,' I said.

'And this is another of the facts of life and equally important. Now, where was I? Oh, yes, under no circumstances, never – and I mean never – grow a moustache alone. People look at a moustache and what do they see?'

'I don't know, Ammar, what do they see?'

'They see a car salesman, they see a charlatan, a swindler, a fraudster, a con artist, a man who is not what he appears to be – so no moustaches.'

I had no idea, at the time, what the word 'charlatan' meant, but I was impressed by the sound of it. I liked the way Ammar said it, the way he made it sound. *Char-la-tan*. It made me think that he knew what he was talking about.

'So, Joseph, you grow a beard that's not too long but not too well kept either. The beard that is too neat and too well trimmed makes people think you're full of your own importance, a spiv. That's not what you want. You want to be seen for what you clearly are – a good worker, a craftsman. Grow a beard that says: "I'm just so busy that I don't have time to shave, and I'm so busy because I'm so good at what I do, and if you give me this work you'll be glad you did; you'll realise you made the right choice." Trust me, you'll never be out of work if you do that.'

So I went home that evening, and I talked to Miriam, and she giggled.

'I've always thought I'd like to kiss a man with a beard. See if it tickles.'

'I might give it a try.'

'Well, if you do, I'll be happy to have you tickle me,' she said, and she came and sat on my lap. We were out on the little balcony that she had turned into a garden. I remember thinking how light she was, like a little bird perched on my knee, and I was so glad I hadn't walked away, so glad she'd come down the streets out of the sun that Saturday morning. I remember thinking how beautiful she was, how sensual. Her breasts were bigger then, and her belly slightly swollen with the baby, and we made love out there on the balcony.

I grew my beard, not too wild, slightly unkempt. And it turned out that Ammar was right. I've never been out of work a day since, other than by choice. In my experience, people look at someone with a beard and, if it's not too long and not too neat, they see a man with brains, a thoughtful man, a man who can navigate or make things or think things through or analyse problems and reach solutions. They see a hundred different men with a hundred different skills, but each of them is an expert in his own field. A wise man was Ammar, and generous enough to share his wisdom.

We settled into life in Egypt. I sold the motorbike and bought a small car. Our flat was in the middle of the city on a narrow lane, away from the harness of the traffic noise. That street was full of traders, marketers and tradesmen. It was an animated and exciting place to live. Miriam made a home of the flat, little touches, a throw here, flowers there, the garden on the balcony, freshly painted furniture.

We went to night classes for fun. We walked to the college together, then went our separate ways, she to a child psychology class, me to a literature class. She wanted to be prepared, she said, for when the baby was older; she wanted to get it right. I wanted to find out about words like 'charlatan', what they meant and where to use them. I love timber, I love where it comes from and what can be done with it, but I love reading too.

A teacher told me once, when I was 12 or 13, that I was as thick and useless as two short planks. I knew then how wrong he was on all counts, that I wasn't thick and that no plank is useless, but I didn't have the confidence or the balls to tell him. Now I did. When the night classes were over, I'd meet Miriam in the college hall and we'd go for a coffee and some baklava and we'd talk about what we'd learned. Mostly I listened and Miriam talked; all these ideas about how we'd bring up the little one. And I'd watch her face, animated and full of love, full of the excitement she'd talked about back in Jacob's Ladder, and I couldn't but be drawn in and swept along by the marvel of it all.

And yet I never questioned Miriam about the event that had started this adventure. I never asked who the father was or why or when. I was happy to be there with her. I was happy simply to be away from her father's arrogance and interference. Glad to be away from her mother's silent connivance in his domineering ways.

And afterwards we'd wander home through the lamplit alleys, overhearing the intimacies and pleasures of other people's lives, laughing at the pointless arguments, embarrassed but excited by the sounds of lovemaking, walking that little bit faster so that we could get home and make slow, gentle love ourselves. Sometimes I wonder if I secretly hoped my own seed would replace the seed that someone else had sown. Stupid, I know, but no more stupid than a hundred other things in my life.

At the weekends we did the kinds of things tourists might do. We sailed on the Nile by moonlight, there were 300 other people on the boat, but that didn't matter; we drove to the beach, and tried to find a quiet place and failed, and laughed most of the way home when we thought of some of the shapes we'd seen on the sand.

'They weren't walking or running,' Miriam said, 'they were perambulating. Is that the right word?'

'I think it's exactly the right word, with ambling,' I said.

'And sauntering,' and we were off laughing again, our voices floating through the open car windows, out into the traffic jams in which, inevitably, we were stuck.

We trailed around museums and galleries; Miriam liked the quietness and the colour and the coolness. One weekend we drove to the pyramids. To be honest with you, I wasn't particularly electrified. First off, the place was overrun by tourists; it was like an anthill, and buses kept arriving and vomiting more and more of them out, all sunburnt arms and egg-white legs and loud American accents.

'We're tourists too,' Miriam said when I complained.

'Yes, in a sense, but we live in the bloody country and work here and pay our taxes here. And we're not talking so loudly that it seems we're trying to call home without a phone.'

She looked at me with that *there he goes again* look and giggled.

But I'm serious when I say the pyramids did nothing for me. I said it to Miriam.

'I don't think James the Block would be overly impressed by these. They're like big heaps of sand thrown up in the middle of the desert. Not impressed. It's a bit like Las Vegas, all these tourists crawling all over the place.'

'Not that you've ever been to Las Vegas!'

'Agreed,' I said, trying not to smile, 'but if I had been, I imagine it'd be like this.'

And that was the pyramids.

When it got into the autumn and early winter, closer to Miriam's time to deliver, I cut back on work, I stopped taking extra hours, weekends and overtime. Ammar was great about that kind of thing; there was never any pressure on me. He and his wife had girls, so he knew the score.

'When you have three, like Rania and me, you'll want all the overtime you can get, Joseph,' he'd laugh. 'Three pairs of shoes wear out together, and of course the next one in line never wants the older one's coat or jeans. Your time will come. Pray that you have boys. They're easier to please when it comes to fashion. But, for now, enjoy. The first baby is the blessing. Afterwards, the work begins.'

He and Rania knew, too, what it was like to be a stranger in a strange country. It was all right for me: I was out working all day, and every site has its way of bringing men together or keeping them apart as the personalities demand. Ammar was good at managing that too. He could spot potential flashpoints and send the men to different areas of the site. I only ever saw him fire one man, and that was for turning up drunk after lunch one day. He tried to get this chap, who was a roofer, to go home and sleep it off, but the man was full of pride and beer, insisting he was fit to work.

'All you're losing is a half-day's pay, but if you climb that scaffold you're finished here,' Ammar said.

'Fuck you,' the man said. 'There's nothing wrong with me. I could walk that ridge in my sleep.'

'There will be if you fall off the roof. The choice is yours, but I'm not allowing you up that scaffold on my site. It's your decision, my friend.'

The man started up the ladder. He was a big enough guy, but Ammar caught him in an armlock, wrestled him down the ladder and marched him to the office. We heard a lot of shouting and then a chair came through the Perspex window – it reminded me of the day I'd faced Miriam's father in the kitchen. A few of us went over to see if Ammar was okay. He was. The roofer was sitting in the corner, very pale.

'I'm not going to charge you for the window,' Ammar was saying, 'and I'm paying you to the end of the week. Now, there's your cards – go.'

And the roofer went, quietly rubbing his arm.

'I'm glad I spotted that,' Ammar said. 'Imagine if he'd got onto the roof and fallen.'

I could see that he was genuinely relieved.

'I've never lost a man on a site yet and I don't want to start now. Joseph, would you board up that window until I get a new sheet of Perspex please?'

Rania would drop in on Miriam during the week, take her to a film, reassure her about the baby, bring round baby clothes she'd made, that kind of thing. Often, I'd come home to find a full meal ready and Miriam would tell me that Rania had delivered it. She was kindness itself.

And then, near the end of the year, the little fellow was born. I remember going up to see him in the hospital. He was in this incubator behind a glass wall. There were lots of children in the same room, and the nurse had to come and point him out to me. He was so small, so frail, and the image of his mother. I was relieved. I remember standing at that glass wall, and all I could think was that he was so beautiful. I'd never have believed, until that moment, I could look at someone so small and have such a huge love for him.

When the time came to take him home, I remember standing outside the hospital and the nurse handed the little fellow to me and I was terrified. Here was this tiny bundle in my arms, weighing nothing at all, and yet I felt the weight of the world on me. What if we weren't able to look after him? What if we did something wrong? What if he got sick? And then I looked at Miriam, pale and tired but smiling in the back seat of the car, and I recognised my responsibilities and the fear went away, or rather I put it somewhere deep inside me and I kept it hidden there for a long, long time.

We settled into our life, the three of us together. And that was good. I went to work in the morning and I came home in the evening, and when the days brightened and the air warmed a little we'd take the little fellow out in the buggy, wrapped up against the world. And we'd stop at the coffee shop near the college for baklava, and the waitress would smile and come and look at him and tell us he was beautiful, or he was growing, or he was the image of his mother, and we'd smile.

The times I loved best were at the weekends when Rania and Miriam went shopping or to the hairdressers or just out for coffee. Just me and the little fellow left in the apartment together. I'd snuggle him up close to me and sing to him, all kinds of songs from my childhood, and now and then a version of 'If I were a carpenter' that I'd adapted for myself.

If I were a carpenter and you were my baby,
would you live with us anyway, me and my lady?

And then, on Sundays, we'd drive somewhere. I had taken to driving so slowly that Miriam would sit in the back and laugh. Once, a cyclist passed us and she laughed so much that I thought she was going to choke. As the summer broke out of spring, we'd push the little fellow in his pram by the sea or out into the countryside. Wherever we went, he went. We two were three, and we three were one. I don't know if I read that somewhere or if I came up with it myself, but I'm pretty sure it was mine, the ramblings of a younger man's mind.

And that's how life went on for two years. The little fellow learned to toddle and then to walk. We thought about buying an apartment, but we didn't. Neither of us wanted to live in the city, and the price of decent houses at the time meant we'd be strangled by a mortgage. So we let it sit. We had this dream of living somewhere in the countryside, somewhere that had an acre or two. Miriam wanted to keep a donkey.

'If you have one donkey, you'll have to have two. They need company.'

'Okay, we'll keep two then.'

I liked the idea myself. I didn't want to spend the rest of my life on the sites. I had ambitions to get into the finer end of the craft, doing work that was slower and more detailed, but that paid better. I wanted to be known for the kind of work that fulfilled the aspirations of the beard.

Miriam's cousin, Liz, kept her up to date with the news from home. Every Wednesday night Liz would ring, and the pair of them could be on the phone for an hour or an hour and a half. On Saturday nights, Miriam would ring Liz, and they'd be on phone for another hour or more. I could never work out what the hell they were talking about, or how they found enough news and gossip to keep them going for that long, but they did. When the calls were over I'd ask Miriam if there was any news, and in three minutes flat she'd tell me who'd married whom and who'd died and who said what about this, that or the other. And it left me wondering how they'd stretched the few bits I'd just heard to an hour or more. When I'd ring my mother we'd have it all said in five minutes, and if my brother answered we'd be wrapped up in two and still get all the essentials in. Horses for courses, I suppose.

That's how the weeks and months and years passed. We went on holidays, worked, made dinner for friends or went to friends' houses for dinner, did the things people do when they're living their lives. I'd sometimes come in from work and Miriam would be standing at the kitchen table, or I'd catch sight of her on the balcony outside, bending over the flowers in her blue jeans and her tight white T-shirt, and I'd be shocked and excited by how beautiful and sexy she was, how deeply I was in love with her and how much I wanted her. Sometimes, when the little fellow was asleep and the street was quiet, we'd turn off the apartment lights and make love on the balcony, the occasional low jabber of conversation passing on the pathway below, and we'd hold our breaths and remember the nights when we were the night walkers and we'd smile. Miriam's teeth would sometimes bite into my shoulder to keep from crying out when she came. Afterwards, we'd lie in the warmth of the summer city night and whisper quietly about how blessed we were to be together, all three of us.

One Thursday night the phone rang and it was Liz, telling Miriam that her father was dead. He'd come in for his lunch at 2 o'clock that afternoon, as he did, on the dot, every day. He was sitting at the table, wolfing his way through his food as he did every day, when *bang*, he fell forward, face first, into his soup and died, as he'd lived, with his mouth and his belly full. I can't say I shed any tears.

I rang Ammar and he told me to take as long as I needed. We packed up the car, put the little fellow in his seat and headed for the border. The minute we crossed it, out of Egypt, I got this knot in the pit of my stomach. Partly, I knew, it was because we were heading back to the roadblocks and searches, the hassle and the uncertainty of life in a country that couldn't ever seem to find itself or its place in the world. But it wasn't just that, and I knew this.

We were also heading back to Miriam's home, and the last time I'd been there I'd punched her father in the mouth and broken his teeth. We were now returning for his funeral, and I had no idea what kind of reception I was about to get. I certainly didn't imagine that the red carpet would be out for us or that we'd be welcomed with open arms.

But, to my surprise, I got it all wrong. There was such a fuss about the little fellow, the first grandchild, and so much oohing and aahing over him that everything else seemed to have been forgotten. It was like we were the centre of attention and the funeral was only a sideshow. The other thing was that Liz had a little fellow around the same age, and the two kids got on like a house on fire. To be honest, it was one of the best weeks of my life. We had a wonderful time, and we caught up with the old crowd. James the Block came to the burial, and afterwards, when we went back to the house for something to eat, he entertained us with long stories about women and the Gouger and the sites he'd been working on, and he assured me, through half a dozen glasses of wine, that he'd come and visit us in Egypt. I knew he never would.

And then it was time to head back. I was putting our bags in the car on the morning we were due to leave when I heard this voice at my shoulder.

'I wanted to talk to you.'

It was Miriam's uncle, her father's brother. I turned and nodded. He was a damn sight bigger and broader than his brother had been.

'I wanted to talk to you about what happened the last time you were here.'

'Yes.'

'About what happened between you and my brother?'

I nodded again, and tried to keep one eye on his fists while not looking shifty.

'I wanted to say ...'. He was hopping from one foot to another, like a man who had something else on his mind. I took a step back and found my legs pressed against the side of the car, not a great place to be. As I considered my options, he took a step forward. There was nowhere left for me to go. His mouth opened and closed without a sound coming out. For a second I had a flashback of Miriam's father's mouth opening and closing, spitting its contents into my face on the day we'd left this town.

'I just wanted to say ... and earlier wasn't the time ... with his burial and all ...' the words came fast and loud now, too loud, 'I just wanted to tell you that what you did when you hit him that day... it was the best thing anyone ever did to him. He was always a bully, right back to when we were kids. Always telling people how to live their lives and what they should and shouldn't do. I only wish I'd had the courage to do what you did years before. I just wanted to say that before you go.' And then he shook my hand and smiled and walked away. I felt ten feet tall. I was thrilled that someone else understood why I'd done what I'd done. I remember thinking that I wouldn't fit into the car; I was feeling *that* pleased with myself. I think I must have smiled all the way back to the border and beyond.

We settled again into life in Egypt. I went back to working on the site and Miriam returned to doing the things she did, bringing the young fellow to the park, meeting her friends, looking after the apartment. She had enrolled in an accountancy night class a few weeks before her father's death, so she got back to that too.

One evening, about three weeks or a month after her father's funeral, I came home from work and I was sitting at the kitchen table, feeding the little fellow, trying to get him to eat his vegetables, playing one of the usual games I played when it came to anything green, flying the food on a spoon through the air.

'Here's a plane coming in, all the way from America. Flight 816 – we need to land urgently – low on fuel – come in, Cairo airport – please open the airport.' And his mouth opens and the flight lands and he chews it up. 'Oh no, the plane, the passengers, the crew, all gobbled up by the airport monster,' and he laughs heartily, and then the next flight of vegetables comes in and so the game goes on until his plate is cleared or he loses patience with the incoming planes and spits one out, and all subsequent flights are cancelled.

For some reason I glanced across to where Miriam was standing, leaning in the open doorway to the balcony and, whatever way it was coming in, the light caught her eyes and I saw that she was crying.

'You're not happy here, are you?' I said.

Her shoulders rose and tightened, but she said nothing.

'You want to go back home, don't you?'

She nodded.

'I'll talk to Ammar about it.'

And I did. He was, as he always had been, totally supportive.

'I'm never happy to lose a good man, Joseph. I knew the first day you came looking for a start that you'd be a good worker and a gifted one. But we all have times when we need to change direction; decisions have their own explanations, and I respect that. You can go whenever you need to go; next week if that's what you want. You don't owe this company anything. You've never once been a slacker.'

I gave a month's notice. I thought that was only fair to Ammar, and he thanked me. From the moment I told Miriam, I could see her excitement grow; day by day she was more and more animated, but she never once asked me if I wanted to stay.

On my last day on the site, the men came together at lunchtime and presented me with three LPs. I know what they were because I still have them in one of the record cases in the attic. There was *And Then There Were Three* by Genesis; *Darkness on the Edge of Town* by Springsteen and a Boomtown Rats' album. The guy who made the presentation laughed when he handed me the Rats' LP.

'We thought this was a good one to give, considering where you're heading.' The album was *A Tonic for the Troops*. I felt my stomach tighten, but I managed a laugh.

That afternoon, as I was about to leave the site, Ammar put his hand on my shoulder and said: 'Be happy, Joseph. We'll miss you here and I'll miss you as a friend, and I think you'll miss us all more than you're saying.'

When I got home and showed the albums to Miriam, she said: 'That was really nice of the men, really nice. I'll put the albums in the box with your tools.'

The following day we packed everything we had into the car and headed back across the border.

Brand New Key – Melanie

When we got back to Nazareth we stayed with Miriam's mother for a couple of days. I hated being in that house. It still reeked of her father; everything about it seemed oppressive, and her mother hadn't shaken off that air of subservience that seemed to hang around her like the scent of one of those cheap perfumes, an aroma that just isn't right. I knew we'd be welcome to stay, but between Miriam's mother's hang-dog look, the spectre of her father in the unfilled top chair at the kitchen table and the phantom pregnancy-maker whose spirit always seemed to me to be loitering with intent in the open kitchen door, I felt like I was living in a nightmare. I couldn't wait to wake up and get the hell out of the place and into somewhere of our own. I sensed, rightly or wrongly, that Miriam wasn't in the same rush, but then Liz suggested to us that we really should be looking for a place of our own. Miriam always listened to Liz and valued what she had to say, so I grabbed the opportunity and rowed in with the enthusiasm, and by the end of that week we'd found a two-bedroom flat on Sycamore Street, not far from my old haunt.

The day we moved in I got in touch with James the Block, and he found me a start on a site in Zip City. It was like the old days. I'd pick him up or he'd pick me up in the mornings, and off we'd go. He had a place of his own by then. I asked him one morning if he was still in touch with the Gouger.

'I am like fuck,' he said. 'Would you hand-feed kebabs to a shark from a bodyboard?'

Once again, we got on with our lives. I worked, Miriam looked after the flat and the little fellow, and every day she walked up to see her mother. Sometimes, in the evenings or at the weekends, we'd take her out for dinner, or Miriam and Liz and she would drive into

Zip City to a film or a concert and I'd babysit. The plan was that as soon as the little fellow started in primary school, Miriam would go back to working part-time in one of her father's shops. She still called them *my father's shops*, even though they now belonged to her mother. At one stage her mother suggested I might like to work in one of them.

'You'd be out of the elements, Joseph. And it's a much more relaxed lifestyle than labouring.'

I didn't tell her that I wanted a life, not a lifestyle, and that I wasn't a labourer. Miriam stood behind her, chewing on a grin and winking.

'Thank you,' I said. 'I actually enjoy the outdoor life.' But while I was saying it I was thinking of James and his bodyboard and the kebabs and the sharks.

On the way home Miriam laughed about it.

'You got out of that one nicely.'

'Can you see me behind a counter, selling beach balls and hula hoops and Star Wars figures?'

'Don't underestimate yourself, Joseph, it's a lifestyle choice,' she said, mimicking her mother.

We saved everything we could that year. We didn't go on any holiday. Miriam suggested we should take a break.

'False economy,' she said, but I put the figures down on paper. How much we'd save by not going, how much we'd save by my doing odd jobs while the site was closed for a fortnight, how much we'd save if I did some night work for people in the area.

'And will we see you?' she asked.

'I'm doing this so we can get a place of our own as soon as we can.'

'I know that, but we don't have to stop living in the meantime, do we?'

'That's an exaggeration.'

'Maybe. But when I was 8 or 9 my father was working day and night to get one shop up and going, and then a second. He was doing it for all the right reasons: so we'd have a better house, so my mum and me would be well looked after, so there'd be no financial worries. But it began to be a habit with him. And it got so we lived by his rules and the demands of his work and his hours. You saw that yourself. By the time I was 15 he had three shops, and I felt like I had to make an appointment to see him. And it turned him into a complete asshole.'

'I'm not your father.'

'No,' she said, but *not yet* hung in the air, unspoken.

'And we do want a house of our own.'

'Yes, we do.'

'We'll take a few day trips next week.'

'Okay,' she said, and then she asked: 'We're okay, aren't we?'

'Yes,' I said. 'We are.'

Sometimes, in the evenings, Miriam's cousin, Liz, would come down to the flat, and the pair of them would sit at the kitchen table talking. I might be watching TV or reading the paper, and they'd be there chatting away. Mostly I'd be lost in what I was reading or engrossed in a football match on the television, but sometimes I'd dip in and out of the conversation. Mostly it was about the little fellows and how they were doing, who was first on the slide in the park that morning, or who fell off the swing, or which of them had said what clever thing. Or it might be about which shops had a sale in baby clothes. Occasionally, not often but now and then, I'd hear Miriam talking to Liz about what had happened in her mother's kitchen, about the fluffy individual skulking in the doorway, and they'd talk about it as though it really happened, as though it were fact and not a concoction. I envied them that intimacy, and I envied the way they could talk about it as though they believed it had really happened. I envied how Liz took whatever Miriam said about it as gospel. There was no questioning, just acceptance. I'd sit there and I'd pretend to be immersed in the newspaper, but I'd be listening closely, feeling a mixture of jealousy and anger rising in me. Not that I ever said anything to Miriam. I'd think about it, but it always seemed easier to let it go, to put it back inside that unidentified place where I kept that kind of stuff. No point in dragging it out and parading it around the place. It wasn't going to do any good. It never had and never would.

I suppose the other thing I envied was the closeness between Liz and Miriam, not just the family blood running in their veins but the deep friendship between them. They might only be cousins, but they were, to my kind, what sisters should be.

I didn't have anyone that I'd talk to about things like that, and I know damn well that I'm not the only man to find himself in that situation. Fellows don't tend to talk about that kind of stuff, personal stuff. When I'd go out for a few beers with James the Block we'd talk about the kinds of things fellows talk about all the time – football, the weather, work, what we'd seen on the telly or what was in the papers, crap like that.

One Friday night I went out for a couple of drinks with James. We were talking the usual rubbish about work and about the latest football form and that kind of thing, harmless but entertaining. And then we had another few beers and we had a bit of a laugh about the days when we had shared the flat, and we took the piss out of the Gouger *in abstentia*. And then we had another couple of beers, and the next thing I know is James starts telling me about this girl he's going out with up in Zip City.

'I was up with her last weekend, and we went out for something to eat and a few drinks, and then we went back to her place, the way we always do. She went to have a shower and I'm lying there, like a tent in the bed, waiting for her. And then she comes back into the bedroom and she sits on the end of the bed and tells me she wants to talk. Now I don't mind talking, but I have a horn on me the length of a wet week, so I say to her: "Can we talk later, when we're finished shagging?" And she says: "You always fall asleep when we're finished shagging. I want to talk *now*." So we talk. Correction, she talks, and once the monster lies down I try to stay awake and listen. And it's all about putting the relationship on a more solid footing, getting our priorities sorted. It sounds to me like a business plan, but I say nothing. Then we get to the nub, not the rub but the nub, Joey boy. No rubbing that night I can tell you, just nubbing and business plans and marriage and kids. She wants to have kids. And she wants to get started. No more johnnies or pills, just bareback riding.'

'She didn't say that?'

'No, the poetic phrase is mine. But there's no talking to her; it's like putting snowballs in a frying pan.'

I laughed and we went on talking, and I ordered another round of drinks, and then James ordered one, and by then we were pretty pissed. And the next thing I knew I was telling him about Miriam and her story about the feathery guy in her mother's kitchen doorway. It was just such a relief actually to be able to tell someone, just to get it out of my brain, to get to talk to someone about it rather than having it mulling away in my mind. I'm not saying it's something I thought about all the time; I didn't. But neither was it something that never crossed my mind, because it did, regularly. And, like anything you can't talk to someone about, it just wears a groove in your brain, running round and round and never finding any new direction or any way out.

The great thing about telling James was that he didn't laugh. He asked a few questions, and I answered them as well as I could, and then we went on to talking about something else, and it was all just natural. I was sorry I hadn't talked to him sooner, and sorry I hadn't talked to Ammar about it either, but then I told myself there's no point in worrying about stuff like that: what's done is done.

'If my aunt had balls she'd be my uncle,' I said.

Drunk and all as he was, James looked at me as though I had two heads.

'What are you on about?'

'Nothing. Nothing, I was just thinking out loud.'

'Well, if that's the deepest thought you can muster, you might as well keep your philosophy to yourself,' James said, and he sucked the life out of the cigarette he was chewing. We both laughed, and I ordered another round of drinks.

A couple of weeks later we were out again, and he mentioned *the loitering Lothario* story, as he called it. But it was just in passing. He asked me something, and I answered again as clearly as I could, and he said: 'I wouldn't let it get in on me. It's the kind of a thing that could work away like woodworm, and the next thing you know there's nothing left.' And that was it, end of story.

We got back to talking about the woman he was seeing in Zip City.

'I'm nearly afraid to ride her,' he said. 'Every time I do, I'm thinking she's up to something, trying to get herself up the pole.'

He lit a cigarette and drew deeply on it. The tip reddened and blazed, and then he exhaled.

'Tell me this,' he asked. 'Are you and the missus planning on having any more kids?'

'We've talked about it.'

'And?'

'And we decided we'd wait until the little fellow is settled into the primary school and we have a place of our own, a house.'

'What age is Miriam?'

'23.'

'And you're what? 30?'

'28.'

'Only kids.'

He pulled on his cigarette and leaned back in his chair.

'Would you like to have more kids?'

'Yes, I would.'

'Just because you think the little fellow is not yours?'

'I like kids. I'd like to have two or three more.'

'Well don't let your dick rule your brain. Kids have to be looked after and fed and clothed and housed and educated and set up for life. And you get no thanks for it. Five minutes of pleasure for responsibility beyond measure, isn't that what they say?'

'You're not anxious to have any yourself then?'

'I'd rather have a hot poker shoved slowly up my sphincter. Twice.'

There was a foreman on the site where James and I were working. He came from somewhere up the north of the country. His name was Paul. I can't remember his second name – I think I've just blocked it out of my mind. He wasn't a nice man, and that's putting it mildly. He gloried in making people look stupid. He was a born bully. The only one who seemed to get on with him was James, and I put that down to two things. Paul was afraid of James's tongue; he was sharp himself, but not a patch on James, so he didn't get on to James because he'd never want to be seen to be coming out second best in any argument. The other thing was that he and James would go drinking now and again, not often but from time to time.

Paul had this habit, at lunch hour or during tea breaks, of coming and plonking his boot on the side of a barrel or a cavity block or wherever someone was sitting, and once he did that you just knew he was either going to give them a bollocking or sneer and jeer at them.

It was a lunch hour, about six weeks after our night of drinking. All the plumbers, brickies and carpenters were sitting in a circle in the open air, a beautiful, warm early summer day with the sunlight sweeping through the open windows of the houses we were finishing. I knew Paul was behind me by the shadow that fell across the side of my face, and almost immediately the chap beside me shuffled a few inches to his right and the boot fell on the plank, and my flask wobbled and settled.

'Having a bit of trouble with getting the stairs into number 71 are you?' he asked, and I could hear the snide tone in his voice.

'It's tight enough, but I'll get it done.'

'I'll send someone down after the dinner hour to get the job finished properly. A bird never flew on one wing. Isn't that what they say?'

I was silent. That was the trick with Paul: listen, keep your mouth shut, let the storm blow over and then get on with your work. There was nothing he liked better than for some unfortunate to stand up to him; he'd get weeks of bullying and sarcasm out of that.

'I want you to make sure you have it done, and done properly, before you leave. There's a client coming to look at that house this evening, I want everything shipshape in there. No half-measures, no corners cut. This is a cash customer, and cash is king in the current climate. You're not flying off anywhere in a hurry, are you?' I could imagine him smirking above me, his breath warm on the side of my face.

'No, I'll be here till it's done.'

'Wise man this, knows what side his bird seed is buttered on.'

And then he wandered away, ambling down the site, whistling a few bars of 'Stairway to Heaven'. The general conversation resumed, but then I heard his footsteps behind me again, and a moment later the boot landed beside me for a second time. For a moment there was silence. I looked up. Paul was surveying the assembled workers, and everyone knew there was something coming.

'Tell me this, boys,' he said slowly. 'How would you know someone was after having oral sex with an angel?'

There were guffaws from some of the men. The boot remained planted on the plank beside me. I knew Paul was working his audience, milking the moment for all it was worth. This was a performance in search of an audience.

'You'd know by their cough,' he said at last, and with that I turned to see him bring his closed fist to his mouth, cough, and in the same moment open his fist to send a handful of feathers floating through the air. The place erupted with laughter and knee-slapping, and the hilarity went on and on. Only two people weren't laughing. One was me. The other was James the Block. He was seated just across the open ground from where I was, and he had this face on him like a traffic light – green, yellow, red, green, yellow, red. I looked at him and I thought, you bastard, you fucking bastard. I said nothing, but there and then I made up my mind about two things. Firstly that I was never going to drink again, and secondly that I was going to hand in my notice that day. But I said nothing, just sat it out till the end of the lunch hour, and then I told Paul I was leaving, and I made sure that everyone heard what I said.

'But you can't do that,' he smirked. 'You can't just walk off a site like that. You have to work your notice. You'll lose your pay.'

'I don't care.'

Suddenly, things weren't so funny any more.

'And what about the stairs in number 71? There's the customer calling tonight. Who do you think is going to finish that?'

Now it was my turn to savour the moment. I shrugged as though I were reconsidering.

'I'll tell you what,' I said. 'Why don't you get Led Zeppelin in to finish it?'

With that I walked off the site, and I have never worked a solitary day on anyone else's building site since.

Never Been to Spain – Three Dog Night

I wasn't sure how Miriam would react to what I'd done. I couldn't tell her the whole story – how I'd talked to James about the stranger in the kitchen doorway episode – and I couldn't tell her about the foreman's joke at my expense, because ultimately it was at her expense. So I had to talk to her generally about how horrible it was to work for him. It wasn't the first time she'd heard me mention his name, so it didn't come as a complete surprise to her. Still, walking out on a well-paid job with nothing obvious with which to replace it, and at a time when you're saving to buy a house, is not something that will necessarily go down well at home.

But I was pleasantly surprised. Miriam listened, nodded and smiled. And then we sat out in the little yard at the back of the flat, she brought out tea and k'nafeh, and we sat and talked about the future and about us.

I found myself listening and watching her as she talked. Everything she said was positive and supportive, and not once did she mention the offer her mother had made for me to work in one of the shops.

'This is an opportunity,' she said. 'Take a few days, think things over. We won't starve. It's a chance to look at what you want, at what we want. You weren't meant to spend your life on a building site.'

'That's what I've been thinking.'

'Good. There are lots of ways to make a living. You're a talented man, Joseph. And we're a damn sight better off in every way than we were when we left for Egypt. You'll do just fine; work has a way of tracking down a craftsman. And you might even consider all the other things we haven't done – apart from work. All the places we haven't been, all the plans to travel. I'm not saying we should do it now, but it's a good time to make a plan, isn't it? It's a chance to look forward, to get our priorities right.'

I watched her, sitting across the garden table from me, her eyes full of life and her smile drawing me in and on, and I marvelled at her enthusiasm for the ordinary. James the Block, the fucker, had been right about one thing – we were young and we had our lives ahead of us. Miriam was beautiful and sexy and sensual, and I'd almost forgotten that in the day-to-day routine of working and travelling and sleeping – the things we call survival.

We had a lot of sex that week, when the little fellow was at school and when he went to bed and before he woke up in the morning. We made love in bed and in the kitchen and on the stairs and in the car and, once, while the woman next door was at the market, we made love on the timber deck in the small back yard. The sun was beating down and the wood was hot under my skin, and Miriam was a silhouette, like the shadow she'd been on that early morning outside the other flat. But this time she was there above me, the transparent sky and the sunlight were white and yellow auras about her clean, blonde hair. The tanned skin on her shoulders was the richness of the earth, and when she rolled off me and lay naked on the slatted boards, her hand in mine, the freckles on her face were tiny, dark roses opening to the heat of the day. I was so happy that I'd left the site, and happy to have those days together.

At the end of the week, Miriam went shopping with Liz to Zip City. She brought me back an album: *Long Distance Voyager* by The Moody Blues.

'I know you like them, and I thought the title was appropriate.'

'I do like them, and yes, it is. I'd better get off my backside and find some work.'

'You will. I know you will.'

I did what most people do when they're out of work. I went around and put up cards in shop windows, and I pinned posters on the notice-boards in the supermarkets:

Handyman/carpenter available for work.
No job too big or small. Call to 13 Sycamore St – 10 pm – 6 pm.
Top-quality work. Keen prices.

'You didn't say you're a craftsman.' Miriam said.

'No, I think that would put people off; they'd think I was too expensive. Plus, it cuts down the kind of work you get offered.'

'And you didn't put your name on the notices.'

'No.'

She nodded. She didn't need to hear me say I'd been ashamed.

Late one evening, at the end of the following week, a man arrived at the house. He was wearing a duffel coat – something I hadn't seen in an age – and he had this habit of shrugging while he spoke; it made him look uneasy, shifty even.

'Do you think you might be able to make me a set of bookshelves?'

'I might,' I said, and it took all my willpower not to laugh.

'Nothing too fancy, just plain bookshelves along one wall.'

'I understand.'

'Have you done any carpentry?'

'I have, yes. I'm a qualified carpenter.'

'Right.'

'Great. I'll be down to you in the morning, first thing.'

'Just simple shelves,' he said, turning and shrugging again.

To his surprise, I believe, the shelves went up quickly and stayed up.

'You're handy at the timber work.'

'Thanks.'

'Do you think you'd be up to putting a built-in wardrobe in my daughter's room?'

'I'll give it a shot,' I said.

Miriam was amused and then annoyed.

'Did you not tell him you're the best at what you do? That you've worked here and abroad? That you had fifteen men working for you in Egypt?'

'No point,' I laughed. 'All he's worried about is that the shelves stay up and the wardrobe doesn't fall down. I could use six-inch nails to keep them in place and he'd be just as happy. In fact, I think he's disappointed that he can't find a single nail in any of the work I've done.'

And that's how it started. The following week, a friend of the shrugging man asked if I could build a fitted kitchen, and then someone else wanted a garage built, and it went from there – making a table, replacing

windows, reroofing, extensions, renovations, my first house. By the following summer I had two guys working with me. They're the same two
men who are still with me today. I remembered something else Ammar
had said: 'Never let your business get too big, Joseph, and you'll never go
out of business.'

In the early spring of 1983 a house came up for sale on Woodbine Street
and, of course, we had to go and have a look at it. It was a cottage, but
Woodbine Street is a nice place, a wide street with good space to the front
and huge gardens at the back.

I remember driving down one evening to see the house. We were
determined not to show too much interest to the estate agent, but we
were both tired of living in flats. We'd been together for seven years, and
we'd never had a place that was ours. Apart from the short time sharing
with Miriam's mother, we had never even lived in a house.

When the agent described the cottage as being *in need of some repair,
but a blank canvas on which potential owners can put their own stamp*, she had one
foot on the line between understatement and lies. It was a kip. The roof
was sagging like an old man's trousers, there was no running water, no
electricity, the floors were rotten and the garden was a jungle.

While we stood on the back porch the estate agent twisted and turned
several keys in the rusted lock – the front door had been nailed up to pre-
vent undesirables using the interior for disagreeable activities, she said. I saw
Miriam stifle a grin, and I resisted the urge to tell the estate agent that they
needn't have bothered going to the trouble and point out to her that there
wasn't a pane of glass in any of the windows. In the end, I couldn't resists.

'I think there's something moving down there,' I said.

'Where?' She jumped back from the still unopened door.

'Down there.' I pointed into the forest of briars and overgrown
shrubs.

'Really? What is it?'

'I suspect it's the last living dinosaur,' I said. 'It's probably been living
there for three centuries, undisturbed.'

'Don't mind him,' Miriam said. 'He has a warped sense of humour.'

Eventually, we got inside and walked through the three downstairs
rooms, scattered with empty beer cans, broken bottles and used condoms.

'I'm very, very sorry,' the agent said to Miriam. 'I understood this place had been cleaned up … cleared up … cleared out before we came here. I apologise.'

Neither she nor Miriam was willing to join me in my cautious climb up the unstable flight of steps. Upstairs there were three rooms. Two were empty, the third housed a mattress, a collection of porn magazines, enough beer cans to wallpaper a brewery and an orchard of fruit-flavoured condoms.

'It needs a bit of work,' the agent said, after I'd abseiled back down the stairs.

'You could say that.'

'But structurally it's sound. Mostly, it just needs redecoration and a bit of TLC.'

'You haven't been upstairs,' I said. 'Roof, stairs, floors, water, sewage, electricity, plastering, fitting a kitchen, replumbing, putting in showers, new doors and windows and a couple of skips to clear it out.'

The estate agent coughed uncomfortably.

'How much?' I asked.

'Cash is king in the current climate,' the agent smiled.

'Now where have I heard that before?'

She named a price. I offered one-fifth of what she'd asked. She laughed. The following morning she called to the flat to tell us that the seller had agreed to accept our offer. She wasn't laughing then.

'She said she had put in a good word for us because we were nice people.' Miriam told me after she'd walked the agent to her car.

I spent every spare hour I had for the rest of that spring and summer working on the cottage. The two guys who were working with me put in weekends and evenings without ever asking for a cent. It was a bigger job than even I'd imagined. Effectively, I was building a new house within the four walls that were standing. But I got it done – we got it done – and by summer's end the place was habitable and we moved in. Half-finished floors, a maze of paint tins, walls unskimmed, but it was ours, our house, our home.

The day we moved in, I gave Miriam a gift of the Eurythmics album *Sweet Dreams*. I chose it because she loved the band and because it had the track 'This is the House' on it. Little did I know how ironic that was to become. And neither did I realise that the album had a track called

'I've Got an Angel' on it. Sometimes, when it came on the record player, Miriam would smile at me and I'd say nothing. She bought me a copy of Crosby, Stills, Nash & Young's LP *Déja Vu*.

'Because it has "Our House" on it and because you've been wanting a copy of it for years.'

Hers was the better choice.

Son of My Father – Chicory Tip

*A*part from the cottage itself, there were two things I really liked about this place. The first was the garden. It has this huge area stretching down to a little stream that ran along the back boundary. Not a garden that would feed a donkey, but a very fine garden by any stretch of the imagination. And the other thing is the workshop. The minute I threw my eye on the place, that was what really caught my attention, a fine, big space. Once the renovation was done on the house I got cracking on it, and turned it into a workshop where I could work at night, doing bits and pieces of furniture-making. It's a bright space with everything organised the way I like it. I built a little bench inside the door where people could sit while they were waiting to collect stuff or going over plans with me. The front window, where I have my workbench, looks out across the yard, so I can see who's coming before they see me. The side door faces the back door of the house – I couldn't have planned it better if I'd built it myself.

By the summer of 1984 the business was up and running. The van I had at the time was pretty clapped out, so Miriam and I talked about getting a new one – not brand new, just new to us. I've never bought a new car or van in my life. I was a bit uncertain about it. I don't like borrowing, and we were in hock for the house. My own inclination was to get the van I had patched up, but Miriam had the opposite view.

'Get the newer van. What will people see? They'll see a builder on the up. They'll see someone who's doing really well. Keeping the old one is a false economy. You're putting good money after bad into it.'

I had to admit that she had a point. We went from that to talking about putting the business on a firmer footing, setting up a company, getting registered, doing things properly. I remember the evening well;

we were in the workshop and the big sliding door was wide open and the evening sun was streaming across the floor and lying up against the workbench at the window. We were standing there, and the little fellow was playing in the corner and we were trying to come up with a name for the would-be company. At first it was a game, and we were suggesting the most ridiculous names we could think of, nonsensical names like The Hammer and Saw Construction Company or the No Nails Ltd or The Toothless Saw Conglomerate.

'We need something that sounds reliable but modern,' I said.

'I think what you really need is something strong and macho,' Miriam said, and then she dropped her voice so the little fellow wouldn't hear. 'How about Cocks with Blocks?'

'Or The Hammer Men.'

'Or The Vice Squad.'

We fell around the place laughing, but eventually we got back to trying to find something that was snappy and easy to remember. But we just kept on hitting a brick wall. In the end, the little fellow looks up at us and he says: 'Why don't you call it CCaR.'

It sounded good to me – short, catchy – but I had no idea what it meant.

'It means Construction, Carpentry and Renovation. Isn't that what you do, Daddy?'

And he was right; he'd hit the nail on the head. I remember thinking it was an inspired name – short, sharp, saying everything that needed saying.

'That's brilliant,' I said. 'Isn't that brilliant?' I turned to Miriam. Her face lit up with pride. I mean, the little fellow was only 8, going on 9, and he'd come up with this snazzy name. Miriam winked at me, and I winked back, and then the little fellow winked at both of us. There was no getting past him with anything.

About three weeks after that I bought the van, but I said nothing to Miriam or the young fellow. Instead, the morning I collected it, I left it in with a friend of mine who does sign painting, shop fronts, stuff like that. I got him to paint the two sides of the van, and that evening I drove it into the yard. Miriam and the little fellow came out to meet me as usual, and there was such a great fuss about the van. It was the little fellow who noticed the side panels first, and then the excitement! I'd never seen anything like it.

'Look, Mammy, look, look, look, look,' he shouted, and he dragged her around one side of the van and then the other to show her, there in bold, big red letters was CCaR. And under that, in fancy italics, *Construction, Carpentry and Renovation*, and under that again our phone number. If the young fellow was excited, I could see that Miriam was almost delirious. I could nearly hear what she was thinking: that this was the first step and we were on the way up.

I sent a picture of the house and workshop, with the van outside, to my mother, and another invitation to her to come down and stay with us. She wrote back to say it all looked lovely and wishing us well, but saying she was too old to be travelling all that way and that we had enough to be doing without looking after her. She'd shown the photograph to my brother, and he put a p.s. on the letter saying how proud the old man would have been to see how well I was doing. I liked that.

We'd drive up twice a year to see my mother, sometimes the three of us or sometimes just me and the little fellow, and then stay overnight, or at most for two days. We'd go up to the cemetery, and the neighbours would come in and tell me I must be doing really well and what was it like to be living in Zip City and I'd tell them that we weren't in the city, that the town was seven miles outside it and they'd nod and say it must be exciting all the same, being that close to so many great things and there must be something different to do every night.

If only they'd known. The truth was that our lives were much like theirs. Miriam was working part-time in her uncle's shop. He'd bought her mother out. I was building and renovating during the day. Often the jobs were hours from home, and most evenings I was in the workshop making the things that really paid – tables, chairs, dressers, kitchen units – everything handcrafted. We were getting on with our lives in the same way they were getting on with theirs. Their kids were growing up, and our little fellow was growing too. Himself and Liz's young fellow were mad into football, and more often than not the van was on the road at weekends, bringing the under-10 and later the under-12 teams to matches in towns and villages across a forty-mile radius. Sometimes we'd get pulled over by the army, but generally, when they saw a dozen kids sitting on home-made wooden benches in the back of the van, already dressed for the match ahead, they'd wave us through.

And that's how we got on with our lives for the next couple of years. Work, football, school meetings, holidays, family visits, all the things that make up a great part of what we call a life. We were still young – I was in my mid-30s, Miriam had just turned 30. We had energy and we were always on the go. Business was good. Life was good. We were still in love, and sometimes, late at night, after we'd had sex or when we were driving home from a concert or something like that, we'd talk about the possibility of having another child. Back then, I still believed it would happen. I can't remember when I stopped believing. But I'd see Miriam in those jeans and a tight white T-shirt and I'd want her; I'd really, really want her.

My mother died in January 1988. My brother found her sitting on the bottom step of the stairs with the phone in her hand. That's where she always sat when she was on the phone. We'd offered to move it into the kitchen or the sitting room, but she wouldn't hear of it.

'I like sitting there when I'm on the phone. I can see what's happening on the street.'

'But nothing ever happens on the street,' we'd told her.

'You'd be surprised.'

'Well obviously it only happens when Joe and I are away,' my brother had said.

'You'd be surprised,' she'd said again, and that was that.

And that's where he found her. The doctor reckoned she'd been dead for eight or ten hours. My brother rang Miriam, and she got word to me. I came home immediately. She already had my bag packed, but only mine.

'We're two people down in the shop, and besides, I don't think it'd be good to take you-know-who out of class. He has tests in three weeks, and this is his last year in primary school.'

'I think a boy should be at his grandmother's burial,' I said. 'Heaven forbid, if your mother died, I'd want him at that funeral. So would you.'

'That's different,' Miriam smiled. 'That would be here in town. You're looking at a day getting to your mother's house, one or two days for the funeral and a day to get back. That's almost a week gone.' She sighed deeply and shook her head. Her eyes were wide and bright, beautiful and cold.

'Very well,' I said.

'If this were holiday time … it would be different.'

It was a long drive from here to my home place, long hours on the road, two coffee stops. Some of the time I thought about Miriam's decision. I was angry. There'd been no discussion. I knew she had never really warmed to my mother. The last time we'd been to see my mother as a family had been two years earlier, and on the way home, with the little fellow fast asleep on the back seat, we'd had words about my mother.

'Why do we always have to traipse up here? How come she's never once come to see us? It'd be a lot easier than dragging a 10-year-old halfway across the country,' Miriam had said.

I'd tried to explain. 'She's never been more than fifty miles from home. She was born in the village, lived in the village, and will no doubt die and be buried in the village.'

'That's not the only point,' Miriam had said. 'She has no …'.

'No confidence?'

'No, not confidence. I wish you wouldn't finish my sentences for me.'

'Apologies.'

'She has no manner, no social skills, no willingness to open to people, no sense of exploration.'

I remember thinking, in that moment, that all of us are the shavings of someone else's piece of wood, and none of us falls far from the ones who made us. I found myself thinking of that first conversation with Miriam's father on the night of his birthday.

'Taciturn,' Miriam said at last. 'She's taciturn.'

'I think that's being a bit hard on her. She's shy.'

'Introverted, distant …'.

'Oh come on, Miriam.'

'And she's cold.'

I knew, then, that there was no point in arguing.

So I thought about that, but none of the things Miriam had said made it any easier to be driving back alone to my mother's funeral, and yes, I was very, very angry.

After the first coffee stop, I tried to put my anger away and recollect the moments in my mother's life when she had been happy. I searched for the remembered smiles, but I had to go back a long way, right to before my father's death, to the four of us driving in my brother's Chevrolet, back to a birthday when my father had bought her flowers and a necklace and taken her out to dinner and my brother had wondered, after they'd left for the restaurant, if my father was shagging someone else. I was 12 and my brother was 18, and I had no idea what he was talking about.

'When was the last time he took her out to dinner or bought her flowers?'

'I don't know.'

'Me neither. That's my point.'

I still had no idea what his point was.

'I wonder who she was calling,' my brother said. We were driving to the undertakers to choose a coffin. 'If someone had rung her, they'd have noticed she'd gone silent.'

'True.'

'Unless, of course, it was Mrs Nassir. You could die ten times and she'd never stop talking long enough to notice.'

'True, too.'

We pulled into the undertaker's yard.

'I was thinking about her on the way up here.'

'Yes.'

'She had a pretty hopeless life, didn't she?'

'I guess so.'

'Factory work, marriage, two kids, housework, losing Dad, death.'

'Nine kids,' my brother said.

'What?'

'Two stillbirths before I was born; four stillbirths between you and me; one the year after you were born. Thirteen years, nine pregnancies, two living kids, seven born dead, the massacre of the fucking innocents. No wonder her life was hopeless. And then the hammer man goes and blows his head off. Maybe she'd have been better if he'd blown his balls off years before.'

'I never knew any of this.'

'Neither did I until yesterday.'

'Who told you?'

'The aforementioned Mrs Nassir; she sat me down and told me the whole story.'

'Fucking hell.'

'Couldn't have put it more succinctly myself.'

We buried my mother with her husband and children. I stood at the graveside and tried to imagine what it must have been like for her every time she'd come up to the cemetery, knowing what she knew: that the small parcel of land, the only land my parents had ever owned, was the burial place of so many splintered dreams.

That night I rang Miriam and told her I was staying for the rest of the week.

'The guys were wondering when you'll be back. There are jobs on.'

'I know that. Tell them to get stuck in themselves. They don't need me on their shoulders like a guardian angel all the time.'

Silence.

'We need to get things sorted here.'

'Right.'

Normally, I'd have risen to the challenge of that monosyllable, explained myself, apologised, tried to put things to rights. This time I didn't even try.

'We have things to do.'

And we did. We went to the lawyer and I signed over my share of the house to my brother.

'You should perhaps consider this for a period of time,' the lawyer said.

'No consideration needed.'

'Well an agreed price then.'

'There won't be a price. I have my own house,' I said. 'This house is my brother's house now.'

The lawyer shrugged and said: 'Every transaction merits consideration.'

I was tempted to say the phrase sounded like something you'd find in a fortune cookie, but I kept my counsel.

We cleared my mother's clothes from her room. We offered what was wearable to Mrs Nassir and the other neighbouring women. They took bits and pieces, scarves, a jacket, a coat, two hats. The rest we burned in a barrel in the small backyard. My brother had plans for the house. He had made various drawings and sketches over the years, but each time my mother had said: 'It's fine the way it is. You and Joseph can do as you will when I'm gone.' So here I was, looking over plans, measuring, suggesting, discussing.

'I want to pay you a fair price,' my brother said one night. 'The house was ours, not just mine.'

'I have a house,' I said. 'You've been looking after things here for years.'

'I'd still like to pay you.'

'Okay,' I said. 'I'll tell you what you can do; you can buy me a good dinner tomorrow night. We'll drive somewhere and have a nice meal and that'll be it.'

'Thank you,' he said. 'And there'll always be a room here for you.'

'Meaning?'

He shrugged and smiled a listless, washed-out smile. He looked tired.

'Because I'm here alone for the funeral, you think I might need a bolthole?'

He shrugged again, and then I explained why I was on my own and how angry I was.

'These things happen. Far be it from me to come between a man and a woman.'

And that was all he said about the matter. I said nothing about his disastrous marriage and his wife living in a town forty miles away. I suppose because that's the way I deal with things, or don't, most of the time.

I got back home three days later. It was mid afternoon when I drove into the yard and sat for a moment, giving the ghosts of my home town, who for some unknown reason had travelled with me that day, time to slip out the back of the van before I went inside. I hadn't been surprised that my mother's ghost, and so my father's, had come with me, but I had been more than surprised that there were others there as well. Young men and women I'd gone to school with whose bodies had ended up on the floors of bar-rooms or in hospital beds or in the battered, misshapen wrecks of roadside steel. They'd had their say and told the rags and bones of their unnaturally short stories. So I sat there, waiting for the last of their shivering words to fall silent, the last of their dead lives to seep back to the place on the side of a distant, weathered hill where they'd all been buried till that day.

I opened the back door of the van, half expecting a rush of smothered words and rotting rags, but everything was as it should have been. My toolboxes in place, my weekend case on the floor, nothing out of order, not a sign of the lifeless passengers I'd carried with me through the day. All gone, I thought, and then I smiled and manhandled my bag off the floor and went inside, a knot in my gut. If I'm truthful, that knot had been there from the moment I'd woken that morning. There was something in the air, to quote Thunderclap Newman.

Miriam was in the kitchen. I kissed her on the cheek and put my bag on the floor.

'Don't leave that there,' she said. 'I'm expecting Liz and my mother down any minute.'

'Nice to see you too,' I said.

She laughed, but there was no mirth in the laugh.

'Don't start,' she said.

'Sorry? Don't start what?'

'You went to your mother's funeral. You've been gone almost a week.'

'You knew that.'

'I knew it when you rang and told me you were staying on for an extra four days.'

'What did you expect? That I'd come back the evening of her burial?'

'Don't be ridiculous. No one expected that. I'm just glad no one went with you – a week off school, a week off work. Is that what you planned?'

'School wasn't an issue – as you'll notice, I travelled alone.'

'Oh, so that's what this is about. You stayed away to make your point. Childish!'

'Miriam, what the hell are you saying? I stayed on to sort things out with my brother, to help him clear stuff from the house, to see the lawyer and to have a meal with him.'

'You must have had lots of times for meals. Six days is lots of meals.'

'We had one meal out together. He took me out for dinner the night after we saw the lawyer. The house was left to both of us. I swapped my half for a dinner.'

'That was big of you.'

'It wasn't about being big. It was about his having somewhere to live. We have a house, he doesn't. He was the one who kept an eye on my mother in the past few years.'

'Well, you have a history in that regard, don't you?'

'What?'

'When it comes to being around for parents, you have a history.'

'What are you talking about?'

'Oh, it doesn't matter.'

'It does matter.'

Just then Liz's car pulled into the yard, and Miriam went to meet her.

'Are you around to do the school run?' she asked over her shoulder from the open doorway.

'Yes.'

My mother's funeral wasn't mentioned again for days. The little fellow was thrilled to see me at the school gate, and I took him for an ice-cream. He had a dozen questions about my mother, the burial, what she'd looked like dead, how deep the grave had been, had we seen my father's body in the ground, how cold was a dead body, and was it strange to touch? I realised that he'd never been to a burial, not since Miriam's father died, and he'd been too young to remember that. Strange, I thought; at his age I'd seen lots of dead bodies, been to most of the funerals in my village, learned that death is part of life and that the living should bury the dead.

On the way home from the ice-cream parlour, I called to where the two lads I have working for me, Thomas and John, were out on a job.

'Sorry to hear about your loss,' John said. Thomas said nothing, just shook my hand. That's how they are.

'The job is going okay?' I asked.

'Not a bother,' John said. Thomas had gone back to plastering a wall.

'I'll be down first thing in the morning,' I said. 'Is there anything that needs doing?'

'I left the measurements for the two replacement windows on your bench in the workshop.'

'Thanks. I'll get cracking on them tonight.'

'We won't need them for a couple of days yet.'

'And there were no snags?'

'None.'

'Your man inside wasn't looking for me?'

'Why would he?' John grinned. 'Didn't he have us here? He knows good men when he sees them.'

'True.'

That night, I started work on the replacement windows. It was good to be back in the workshop, good to feel the familiarity of the space, a place for everything and everything in its place. I'd learned that much from my brother. I wanted to ring him, to let him know I was thinking of him, to tell him I hoped everything was going all right and that he wasn't finding the home place too empty, but that would have meant going into the kitchen to use the phone, and I thought it best to leave well enough alone.

At about 9 o'clock the little fellow came out to say goodnight.

'I'm glad you're back,' he said. 'And I'm sorry about Nana.'

'It's nice to be back,' I said. 'And thanks for saying that.'

'Goodnight,' he said, and he hugged me and went back inside.

It was the following weekend. Ironically, the little fellow was over visiting his maternal grandmother. He'd often take off on a Saturday morning if he didn't have football, hop on his bike and cycle over to see her. They got on well; he was an easy young fellow to get on with at that stage, eager to please. I often thought, despite our best efforts to keep things from him, that he had some notions of the stones that were in our shoes. He was forever trying to keep everyone happy, being the go-between even when we thought we'd put a good face on things.

I'm not saying we were at each other's throats all the time. Most days were good days, or passable days. We laughed a lot; we got on with the way our lives were going. I worked hard, I provided well, none of us ever went without the things we needed. Birthdays were always well celebrated. The presents were well thought out. I took time to find things I thought Miriam would like, and she always put thought into the music she bought me for my birthdays. The thing is, I still have most of the albums she got for me – I may have bought the CDs as well, but I still have the albums. When I sit down some nights to listen to music, I'll put on the vinyl and I'll reread the sleeve notes and I'll see the words she wrote at different times. That year, the year my mother died, 1988, Miriam bought me two LPs for my birthday – *I'm Your Man* by Leonard Cohen and *Tracy Chapman*. She said they both reminded her of me. *I'm Your Man* I could understand, but she had to explain that Tracy Chapman's 'Fast Car' could have been written for me and my van. And she was right – it's a great song. I still stick it on when I'm on a long journey, open windows, desert to the left and the right of me, foot to the floor, me in the cab of my van, the road opening out before me, mile after boundless mile.

Anyway, that weekend, the one after I'd come back from my mother's funeral, the one where the little fellow was up with his grandmother, we drove in to Zip City to do some shopping and then we went for something to eat. We sat in the Outside In Bistro. A far cry from Jacob's Ladder, and none the better for it. It's a pretentious kip with glass walls and overpriced food and aspirations *to bring outdoor dining within our invisible walls*. On the few occasions Miriam and I went there I laughed every time a bird crapped on the invisible walls. Miriam thought I was being infantile and told me once that it was time I filed the ball and chain of my working-class background from my mind and got on with living in the real world. Not a great metaphor, I thought, but it put me in my place.

So, that's where we were that Saturday afternoon when she picked up the threads of my mother's shroud and finished that unfinished conversation.

'I've been thinking about your little vacation,' she said, with an emphasis on vacation.

I was lost.

'What vacation?'

'Your week away, your time out with your brother. If you have something to say, if this is an attempt at a statement, I'd prefer it if you had the courage to come clean and say it.'

For a moment I thought she was winding me up, but there wasn't a hint of a smile on her face.

'My time out with my brother, as you describe it, was, in case you need reminding, for the purposes of burying our mother.'

'Some of it was, yes, but only some of it. I have no idea what the rest was about, but I'm guessing, and correct me if I'm wrong, that you were trying to tell me something, to make a point or teach me a lesson. How come, even after twelve years, you can never say what you want to say? If you're bored just say it.'

'What are you talking about, Miriam? I'm not bored. I went home to bury my mother, I sorted the house, I connected with my brother, I clarified the legal situation, I had a meal, I came back, I got on with my work. I was away for five days. When we came home for your father's funeral, we were here for a week – same thing.'

'No it's damn well not the same thing,' she hissed. 'How dare you suggest that! We were up and down to see your mother a couple of times a year. I never saw my father from the day you took me out of here till the day we came back to be at his burial. I could never see him, could never hear from him, never have him come and visit us. So don't put these side by side and expect me to accept that. I didn't see my dad for the best part of three years, you made sure of that.'

'I made sure of what?'

'I wasn't the one who struck him,' she said.

'We left because he was impossible,' I said quietly.

'We left because you said he was impossible.'

'I don't remember you being a prisoner in Egypt. There were no bars on the doors, the phone was there. You knew your way to the Post Office. And the train station.' Even as I said all this, I knew it sounded snide and puerile and her eyes filled with tears.

'What a horrible thing to say.'

'Yes, it was. I'm sorry.'

'I was there because I loved you.'

'And I was there because I loved you.'

'You were there because … oh, who knows why you were there?'

'So this is not just about my mother's funeral?'

'Of course it's not. For heaven's sake, Joseph, when are you going to wake up to what's going on in your life?'

'Soon, I hope, soon,' I said, and then, right on cue, Pickettywitch came on the café music system singing *Same Old Feeling*, with all the angst that only a three-minute pop song can generate.

I paid the bill and we walked to the car and sat in the underground parking lot, and I told Miriam how much I loved her and how beautiful she was and how, every time she passed the workshop door, I wanted her, and how fucked up that time was when we left for Egypt and how young we both were and how the only things I wanted for her were happiness and comfort, and I apologised for her not seeing her father in the years before he died, and she said it wasn't all my fault, and we hugged and she cried and I drove home, fast, and we didn't ring her mother to tell her we were back until after we'd had sex twice.

I tried. I did try. I know that sounds awful – cold, clinical, desperate even – but for the next few weeks, well into the summer, I tried not to be in the workshop all the time. I turned down some jobs; I made an effort to be the man I thought Miriam needed. We did things – as a family and as a couple. We talked, for the first time in many, many years, about having another child. I had this thing in my head about having a daughter.

'We'll see,' Miriam said. 'Let's see how things go. Let's not tie ourselves to deciding today. Is that okay?'

Of course it was okay. It was the first time she'd really given it anything more than a cursory consideration. If I'm truthful, I was elated. And that's how I remember the early weeks of that summer of '88 – a time of possibility and animation and excitement. I was in no hurry – I was 35, Miriam was 30. We were young, everything seemed new. I bought her a jacket that Liz said she loved. I bought her a scarf I thought she'd like. She wore the jacket all the time. She bought me *The First of a Million Kisses* by Fairground Attraction. I thought we were in love again.

The little fellow finished primary school that summer, and we had a couple of months to decide where he might go and what he might do.

We were talking about it one evening in the workshop. Miriam was sitting cross-legged on the workbench, drinking a cup of coffee, and the sun was going down and the evening was golden brown, and I hadn't turned the light on. I was sanding a chair and not really concentrating, and anyway I didn't need to; it was repetitive work. Instead, I was watching the way her hair and the flesh on her neck and shoulder glowed in that late, peculiar light.

'We need to make our minds up,' she said. 'We need to know where he's going, and he needs to know.'

'I thought maybe he'd go to the Tech, see how that works out for him for a year or two.'

She shook her head. 'He's too bright for the Tech. He'll just be frustrated there. He needs somewhere that's going to stimulate him. Somewhere that challenges him and gets the best out of him.'

'I went to the Tech, back in my home town.'

'I know,' she said, and there was something in the way she said it, something in her tone of voice, that chilled me to the bone. If I'd said anything she'd have laughed and told me I was nuts, but I could hear a coolness, a cynicism, a dismissal. 'I think he should go to boarding school,' she said. 'I think he'll love it there, he'll be among like-minded children, he'll be challenged and he'll be stimulated intellectually.'

I pointed out that the Tech had all kinds of academic choices; it had changed from my time when the concentration was on practical subjects. I said I thought he'd benefit from being at home with us for a year or two longer. We talked about it on and off over the following week, and then the decision was made. Boarding school it was.

The day we were due to drive him up to the boarding school in the city, I knocked off work early and came home. When I pulled the van into the yard there was this brand new car parked outside the back door, shiny and bright with an up-to-the-minute reg, straight out of the showroom by the look of it. The first thing that crossed my mind was that someone wanted some work done and was waiting for me inside. But when I got to the kitchen there was only Miriam there.

'Who owns the car outside?' I asked.

'I rented it,' she said.

'You rented it? Why?'

'Well a young boy doesn't want to arrive for his first day in boarding school in a beaten up builder's van, does he?'

I was about to burst out laughing, but I thought better of it. If it had been important enough for Miriam to rent a car then she wouldn't appreciate me laughing about it, so I left well enough alone. Then, when I was putting the little fellow's bags in the boot, I noticed that she had taken the little sticker thing, with the hire company name and logo, off the back window. She wanted the car to look like we owned it. This time I did laugh out loud, but only because there was no one about.

The little fellow gave me a hand bringing out the cases and loading the last of them into the car.

'Well,' I asked, 'are you looking forward to heading off to the new school?'

'Yes,' he nodded. 'I am. It'll be fun.'

'I'm sure you'll make lots of new friends.'

'I hope so.'

I kept a close eye out for signs of doubt or unhappiness, but if I'm honest I didn't see any. He seemed content, not greatly excited, but content nevertheless.

'And you saw your gran this morning?'

'Yes, we went over after breakfast. She gave me lots of money.'

'No harm in that,' I said. 'It'll come in handy.'

Just before we were due to set off, Liz arrived with her young fellow and the two boys chatted and promised to write to one another and to keep in touch. Liz's young fellow was heading to the Tech the following Monday.

On the way into the city, about ten minutes before we got to the school, I said: 'If you don't like it here you don't have to stay. Give yourself a week or two to settle in, but if you're still not happy let us know. Don't just stick it out because you think you have to.'

'I think I'll like it.'

'Of course he'll like it,' Miriam said. 'Why would you put such negative thoughts into the boy's head?'

'I'm just saying, just so he knows and doesn't feel under pressure.'

'No one's under pressure,' she said sharply.

'I think I'll like it,' the little fellow said again, quickly, and I knew it was best to let it go.

So we swept up the driveway and parked our shiny new car right outside and brought in the bags and met the older boys, who showed us to the dormitory. They seemed like nice enough young lads, very mannerly, but then the headmaster was hardly going to send the school psychos out to meet the parents and new boys. It was all brightness and laughter and positive words and warm welcomes. The last I saw of him that day he was standing on the top step, just at the main door, and I could tell he was anxious to get back inside, to get on with doing all the things that were waiting to be done. And I was a little bit jealous. I knew the days of having him in and out of the workshop, the days of driving him to and from football, the evenings of him bringing me out a cup of coffee and a biscuit when I was working, the mornings of dropping him off to school or the afternoons of hearing all the news from his classroom were done and dusted. I remembered from my own school days that, once you move out of the primary system and into the secondary, things change, boys change, even if they don't want to, from little fellows to young fellows, and nothing can stem the tide once it starts flowing.

Then he disappeared back inside and we sat in the car for a minute or two. I didn't know what to say or do and nor, I think, did Miriam. A great sadness had fallen on me, maybe as much for my own losses as for his going away, but I think it was for that too. And then I knew I had to pull myself together.

'Would you like to go for something to eat?' I asked.

'No thank you.'

'Well a cup of coffee then, before we hit the road?'

'No thank you.'

Obviously I hadn't been forgiven for what I'd said about the little fellow not having to stay if he didn't like the school. So off we went with an atmosphere between us that you could cut with a blunt hacksaw. I don't think we spoke three sentences between us all the way home.

The young fellow settled into the school, and we settled into the way our lives were going to be. Miriam was still working part-time in her uncle's shop, doing the books and looking after the orders. She took up a couple of night classes too, in philosophy and Spanish.

'The loving tongue,' I said when she told me.

'I should have known that's the way you'd think,' she said.

I was tempted to add that I'd almost forgotten how it was done, but I didn't.

To be honest, the fact that our sex life was slim to none wasn't all her fault. I was up to my neck in building work, and on top of that, in the evenings after I'd had a bite to eat, I'd head out to the workshop. That's where I was happiest, and that was the work I really enjoyed. Now and again I'd think about giving up the building and developing the cabinet-making. The first time I gave it serious thought I put it off till the little fellow was out of primary school. But once he was in the boarding school, I thought it best to carry on with it, what with fees to pay and all that stuff. I knew I'd do all right at the carpentry, but the money wouldn't come the way it was doing from the building, so I put it on the long finger – again.

Halfway through the young fellow's first year in the boarding school, Miriam told me that the house was too small. She started talking about moving to somewhere bigger.

'Somewhere that doesn't have a van or a truck outside every second house. Somewhere that people actually drive cars.'

Even if they're rented, I thought, but I didn't say it.

I loved Honeysuckle Street; I loved the space we had and the work-shop and the wide street and the room to breathe. I didn't want to move.

'He'll want to bring his friends home with him during the holidays. We need more space.'

'What about if I did some work here?'

'We'd need another bedroom or two, and a new bathroom, and a kitchen that's big enough to entertain in and bright enough to see in.'

'All that can be done,' I said.

'In the never-never of the future?'

'No, I'll draw up some plans this week, let you make whatever changes you want, and then myself and the two lads will get stuck into it. It'll be done before the school summer holidays.'

I turned down two jobs to work on our own place. The two lads and I worked the weekdays, and I went on working in the evenings and at the weekends. Whatever it took to get Miriam the house she wanted was fine by me, once I didn't have to leave Honeysuckle Street. I extended the kitchen and put in a new glass wall, looking down over the garden to the little stream, shades of Outside In. Upstairs, I put in two new bedrooms, a new en suite and a new bathroom. To all intents and purposes, it was a new house – bigger and brighter and fresher – and for a while Miriam seemed happy.

Then she said the garden was a disgrace.

'It looks all right to me,' I said.

'That's because you never look at it; you never spend any time in it. If we're looking out at it every time we sit down to eat, then it needs to be worth looking at. If I hadn't put the flowers and shrubs and trees in, it would still be the way it was when we moved here.'

She was right about that. I rarely went into the garden, seldom stepped farther than the workshop wall. And she had made a lovely job of the courtyard outside the back door of the house. People often commented on it and how colourful it was.

'You have green fingers,' they'd say.

'Not me,' I'd say. 'That's all Miriam's doing.'

And they'd say: 'Well, I wish she'd come down and do mine.'

So, over two weekends, I got a mini-digger in and I dug out a lovely area along the bank of the stream, at the foot of the garden, and built a deck and made good, strong, classy garden furniture. Then I laid some paths and bought in a few mature trees, and by the time the summer holidays came the place was unrecognisable.

During the holidays, the young fellow had some of his friends to stay for a weekend or a week. Sometimes their parents would drop them off, and we always ended up on a walking tour of the garden, and I always listened with a quiet pride when they complimented us on how beautiful it was looking. He was doing really well in school, too, and his reports were all top class. He was happy, there was no doubting that, and Miriam was as proud as punch, which made life easier when I think about it.

She was always talking about him to the neighbours, and sometimes, when Liz came up, I'd feel maybe she should back off a bit about how well our fellow was getting on. Liz's young fellow was in the Tech here in the town, and he was doing all right too, getting along just fine, but she didn't talk about him all the time. It's not that I wasn't proud, but I just felt things needed to be kept in perspective. It's very easy to hurt other people's feelings, even when you don't mean to.

Funny thing is, when I look back on my life, on our lives together, the three of us, and then the two of us when the young fellow was away, I see things that I don't remember happening, even though I know they're true. And I find myself wondering what it is life turns on – for the better or the worse. Does it turn on things as they happened, or is it only afterwards, a week or a month or ten years later, that something slips into place and we take umbrage or we recognise our happiness and the moments in which it was born or established itself in our lives? I often ask myself that question, but I never seem to come up with any kind of answer or anything that might even be the start of an answer. It's a bit like those conversations we mean to have but never do for one sad reason or another.

American Pie – Don McLean

What is it about people in this country – why are we so impressed by foreign accents? About ten years ago I was in a queue in a hardware shop and I noticed that three out of every four people were going to the one assistant. I wondered why, so I stood back and spent twenty minutes watching, listening. From what I could see, it wasn't that this guy was any quicker or more knowledgeable than the other assistants, nothing as obvious as that. He was no better and no worse at his job than any of the other half-dozen people working there. He wasn't more handsome or younger or cheerier. And then it struck me. He was an American, had a foreign accent, and something in our makeup makes us think someone from abroad must know more, must have a view from the bigger world outside, and therefore must be the person we deal with.

So I decided to put my theory to the test. I had two mobile phones, one for work and one for personal calls – Miriam's idea. I started answering the work phone in a French accent. It wasn't a great French accent, but when people can't see you face to face I reckon they're easier to convince. So Gerald was born. He was everything I'm not. He was flirtatious, flighty even, and he'd say things I'd never say in a million years. The drill was this. The phone would ring and Gerald would answer.

'Allo, CCAR, Geral' speaking. 'Ow may ah 'elp you?'

And the caller would give the details of the enquiry and, if it was a woman, every so often Gerald would ask a question or throw in a deep, dark 'Oui', but the way the French say it – *wayh*. Women went mad for it. And now and again he'd say something like, 'You 'ave a most beautiful voice.' He was a cross between James the Block and the Gouger, but more polished. And then he'd say: 'I will 'ave one of our craftsmen call you in the morning. Non, non, because your business is important to us and because you sound so beautiful, I will 'ave our chief crafts-man, Josef, call you at a time that is convenient to you.' But convenient always came out as *konveenyon* and important came out as *im-por-ton*. The number of times he got asked for his number was unbelievable, and when *Josef* turned up to do quotes I'd get stuff like: 'I'll bet Geral' is hot – what age is he?' And the thing was, when women spoke about him, he was always Geral' – never Gerald.

That worked well for almost two years until one day a woman rang and he answered and she spouted away in French, and he hadn't a clue what she was saying and had to hang up. Job lost. So he got the chop and Hank replaced him. Hank is the always smiling, always friendly American. The accent may vary, but the spiel is still the same.

'Hello, CCAR, Hank speakin'. How may I help you? Yes, Ma'am, we sure do. Yes, Ma'am. Yes we sure can. Yes, Ma'am. Let me tell you what I'm gonna do. I'm gonna have one of our craftsmen ... no, I'm gonna have our top craftsman, our number one man, Joseph, call you first thing tomorrow mornin'. He'll come right round and give you an estimate, absolutely free. If I can get your name ... that's a real pretty name. And address and phone number? Yes, Ma'am. And is there a good time for him to call? Yes, Ma'am, he sure will, between 8.30 and 9 a.m. tomorrow. Yes, Ma'am. You have a nice day now.' That's Hank, a lot of *sure do* and *add-ress* and *have a nice day* stuff going on. Hank does the business, but I still miss Gerald; he had a bit of class.

It makes me wonder, though, when people phone me and get an American, do they imagine they're calling a multinational company? And why is it that, when someone comes down here to discuss plans or to pick up a piece of custom-made furniture, they never ask about Hank? Do they think he's working with a hundred other people in an underground fac-tory? Only once has someone enquired about either of my sales assistants, and that, surprise, surprise, was this blonde woman in leopard-skin trousers and a low-cut top who came looking for Gerald and hadn't the slightest interest in the renovation she was supposedly enquiring about. Her house went from three to five and back to three bedrooms in the twenty minutes she was talking to me. In the end, I told her that Gerald had gone back to France to look after his sick father. I never saw her again.

There's another thing that's strange, and it just crossed my mind in the past couple of days. Of all the comings and goings that happened in the years when the young fellow was away at boarding school, there are only three that have really stuck in my mind, and two of them have nothing to do with Miriam or with us as a family. Three events in five years – that speaks for itself, doesn't it?

The first happened one evening in early summer. I was in the workshop doing something or other, and a huge, bells and whistles and two rows of headlamps four-wheel-drive pulled into the yard, and this fellow I vaguely knew came in with a set of plans for a mansion – and there's no other word for it, it was a real *look at me I'm fucking loaded* class of a place. He was building it on the very top of a hill just outside the town. Don't ask me how he got planning permission, because I didn't ask him.

He had the look of Elvis in his Las Vegas period. A white suit and boots and a shirt that was open as wide as a yawning hippopotamus's mouth. Shades in the shape of guitars, hair that was dyed crow-black, and locks that were long and angled. It goes without saying that he had the medallion sprayed against his chest. All that was missing was *Fanfare for the Common Man*.

Anyway, he spread the plans out on the workbench and I realised, straight away, that this was a bigger job than anything I'd ever taken on before, way too big for me and my two amigos. But I wasn't about to tell him that because you never know, and even if you can't be the headliner, you can always be the opening act. So I'm looking at the plans from one angle and then another, playing for time. I'm pointing to this and that, and he's talking about the outdoor hot tub and the sunken lighting in the imported rock face that will run the length of the driveway on one side and the electric gates that'll weigh fifty-six tons or something ridiculous. And I'm thinking that there are two things I can do with this job. I can give a reasonable quote that will satisfy him and make me a few bob, but that will involve subcontracting most of the work and I'll have to be on the job day and night, and if anything isn't up to scratch and the shit hits the fan I'll be the one left carrying the can long after the subcontractors have left the building. Or I can give him a quote that's so high that even he won't go for it, and I'll have my share and my thanks, as the old lady used to say. While all this is going around in my head, I'm still wading through the plans and jotting notes, doing the things people expect, *keeping the customer satisfied*, as Paul Simon said.

Anyway, in the middle of it all, I come across these nine rooms scattered through the house, and I ask your man what they are.

'Bathrooms,' he says, as cool as a cucumber. And he meant bathrooms. These weren't your common or garden en suites. These were full-sized bathrooms, shower, loo, bidet, double sinks, floor-to-roof mirrors, glass-block half-walls, a muck-spreader's delight. And then he goes on: 'Two for the master bedroom, one each for the children's rooms, three for the guest bedrooms and two for occasional visitors.'

I was standing there, listening to this bull, trying to keep a straight face, and remembering that when I had first arrived in this town as a young carpenter, I used to see your man leaping over a ditch or climbing a gate into a field to have a shit, and here he was asking me to build him a house with nine bathrooms.

In the end, the quote I gave him was so high that he got someone else to do the job, and he was happy with what he saw as the bargain, and I was relieved not to have to work on the house. And the funny thing is, the mansion is up there now, plonked on top of the hill, with its sunken lighting that never gets turned on in the man-made rock face, it's unused hot tub in the garden and its three satellite dishes that probably come in handy for drying clothes, and there are three four-wheel-drives outside the front door and not enough petrol to run one of them. I have to admit it: every time I pass the place I smile, and I wonder how they're doing with the paper supplies for the nine bathrooms.

That evening, after Elvis had left, Miriam came out to the workshop with a cup of coffee for me. She saw the plans on the workbench and she was looking at them and I was pointing out the features – including the nine bathrooms and all the attendant accessories – and we were laughing, but I could see that she was impressed by the design, and I could imagine her thinking that a smaller, less ostentatious version would be right up her alley. But, of course, she didn't say anything because she knew I'd laugh, and I didn't say anything because I didn't want her to think I was setting her up.

The second incident is from another summer evening. I was in the workshop, putting the finishing touches to a hand-carved staircase, the kind of job I've always loved. Every time I do that line of work I find myself thinking of Neil Diamond, the *Moods* album, the song 'Morningside', about this old man who makes a table for his children, but when he dies none of them wants it.

Anyway, I was working away, sanding down a newel post. It was a warm evening and the windows and doors were wide open, and for some reason I looked up, and saw this figure coming around the side of the house, down by the gable wall, heading for the workshop. There was something about him that was familiar, but I couldn't put my finger on it, not straight away. He had one of those old-fashioned duffel bags on his shoulder, and his face was red, but not just from the sun.

I have the little bench inside the door, and as soon as this character stepped into the shade of the workshop he dropped his bag beside it and sagged like wet clothes on a line. Down he went with a grunt. I kept on with my work, still not knowing who he was or what he wanted. For a minute or two he said nothing, just sat there, huffing and puffing and trying to catch his breath. Finally, he spoke.

'How's it goin'?'

The moment the words were out, I recognised the voice. I hadn't heard it in ten or twelve years, but I knew it immediately, and as soon as I recognised the voice, I could see the face I'd known, even though it was lost now in another, bigger face, swollen by years of drink and bad eating, all jowls and too much flesh. The man I knew was changed almost beyond recognition, but there was no doubting the voice – James the Block.

I didn't answer him, just got on with what I was doing. He dredged his pockets, one after another, eventually unearthing a half-smoked cigarette. Then there was a search for a box of matches. Finally, he got the cigarette lighting and sucked it deep and hard. Then he held it at arm's length, flicking the ash through the open door and into the yard. I noticed that his hands were shaking.

'I heard you were doin' okay,' he said. 'I heard you built up the business.'

Still I said nothing, just went on sanding the post. He dragged again on the cigarette, sucking it to the very end before crushing the butt beneath his heavy boot.

'I was workin' above in the city the last few years. I don't know if you knew that?'

He paused, waiting for a reply. When none came he continued. 'The thing is, the work is dryin' up, and it's impossible to find a gaff to live in on the money you'd earn. It's like we're back to where we started. The place is flooded with fuckers comin' in from elsewhere, young fellows – the shave, shower and shag brigade. And I wouldn't mind if they were good at what they do. They're not. They're fly-by-nights. And the thing is, they undercut the likes of you and me. And the other thing is that the gaffers on the sites don't give a toss; they just want the quickest work at the lowest price. That's not the way I work, you know that. With me it's full duck or no dinner. So I got the fuck out of there, just landed back here today. Thought I might look for a start in these parts.'

There was a long silence then, followed by the sound of his breathing and a deep, chesty cough. He spat a heavy, leaden spit into the yard.

'But you're doin' okay. That's good. Best move you ever made, goin' out on your own. Wise man.' He held out his shaking hands. 'I know it don't look good, but it still takes two men to keep up with me. I still have it.'

Another silence – this one went on for an even longer time.

'If you hear of anything ...'. He spoke slowly, choosing his words. 'If you know of anyone that might have a start ...'.

I finished the post I was sanding, put it on a shelf and took another from the wooden box beside me. I sensed that James was watching, but I kept my eyes on the work in hand. Eventually, I heard him grunt a couple of times and lever himself up from the bench. Out of the corner of my eye, I saw him lift his duffel bag.

'Right, I can see you're busy ... I'll leave you to it. You have a lot to do. It's good work. And if you hear of anything ...'.

A moment's hesitation, then he shuffled through the open door, dithered again and turned. I saw his mouth open, heard the weight of his breath, waited for whatever it was he wanted to say, but there was nothing. I listened to his feet on the gravel outside, heard the scraping of his boots begin to fade. And then I watched him, framed in the big window, shuffling down by the house and onto the street. I knew why he'd come to see me – he was looking for a start. Not if he was the last man on earth; not if he begged. The bastard.

The third thing, ironically, has to with an Elvis single, 'I've Lost You'. I bought it in 1970. It never really did any damage in the charts, and when I bought it I had no real idea about the depth of loss behind the song. How could I? I was 17. But I bought the single because I loved the tune and I loved the lyric and I loved the way Presley sang it. RCA Victor. Catalogue number RCA 1999. Written by Ken Howard and Alan Blaikley. Horns and strings arranged by Bergen White. Published by Carlin Music. The B-side was 'The Next Step is Love'. I have it all off by heart. Sad but true. Sadder and equally true – there are probably a dozen other singles whose details I could reel off like that. I still have the Elvis one, and it took me years to track down a CD copy of the song. I finally found a live version on *That's The Way It Is*, a 1983 CD release of the 1970 album. All of which has nothing to do with the fact that I seldom play that song any more, and you never hear it on the radio. But, to me, the lyrics are like someone talking to thunder, where he tells about watching his wife sleeping and she's murmuring in her dream. There's a line where he talks about not being able to point out the moment summer turns to autumn or the moment love grows cold. He says the joy is over, but why it's gone neither of them knows. And he knows the morning will bring them back to the mundane – the baby will wake and his wife will stumble sleepily from their room. He has this great line: *In the chill and sullen grey of morn, we play the parts that we have learned too well.* And the song ends with the line: *I've lost you, yes I've lost you, we ought to talk it over now but reason can't stand in for feeling.*

Anyway, one night, somewhere in those years, I finally discovered, or realised, what that song was really about. Another summer night. The few nights I happen to remember from back then seem always to be immersed in late sunlight, the smell of night-scented stock, a moon rising above the stream at the end of the garden, or the street outside the house gradually becoming a ghost road, with occasional warm shadows passing back and forth. That's how I remember it anyway, that's how it still is I suppose.

That night I was finishing up in the workshop and Miriam's gleaming car pulled into the yard and the headlamps caught me standing in the window. I waved into the blinding light and she flashed the heads, off and on and off again. That surprised me. We had reached a stage where we hardly bothered to recognise each other's existence. What surprised me even more was that when she got out of the car she came into the workshop, smiling.

'How goes it?' she asked.

'It's going well,' I said. 'I'm just finishing up for the night. How's Liz?'

'She's well; she said hello.'

'Well hello back, Liz.'

'What are you working on?' I must have looked surprised that she'd asked because she laughed. 'I'm just wondering. Not being nosy.'

'This,' I said, and I pointed to a sketch of a sideboard I'd been asked to make. Nothing too fancy, just a solid piece of work.

Miriam leaned over the drawing. She was wearing a blue halter-neck summer dress, low at the back, and as she bent I saw that one of the clasps on her bra strap was undone. The blue of the narrow band of cloth was bright against her tanned skin, and in that moment I wanted to lean forward and unclasp the second hook. I wanted to feel her skin beneath my fingers, wanted to hear the gentle clip of the hook slipping from its metal eye, to be back in that time when it would have been the most natural and beautiful thing in the world. But, of course, I didn't. I was afraid I'd ruin the moment, that we'd finish the evening fighting, as we so often did. Instead, I stood beside her and we talked about the drawing, and then we talked about Liz, and then Miriam went inside and made some coffee as I locked up the workshop, then went inside too, and we sat across the table from each other and talked the kind of bullshit that had become our staple communication.

Later, I lay awake beside Miriam and suddenly I knew why I'd bought that single twenty years before. Without knowing, I'd bought it for this moment of recognition, this split second of realisation that there was no going back. Everything that was done was done. The Elvis song was like a prophecy, waiting through all those years to be fulfilled. The only difference was that there wasn't going to be any baby waking at six in the morning. Everything has its season, and the season of love and hope and possibility was long gone. We could be pleasant to each other, mostly. We could be circumspect. We could, once in a blue moon, find ourselves making careful love, but the rest of it was gone.

School's Out – Alice Cooper

*T*he young fellow finished in the boarding school in the summer of 1994. He came out of it with flying colours and got a place in the university. The plan was that he'd train as a teacher.

He spent the summer working with me. And he was a good worker. I won't say he was a natural when it came to things like carpentry or plastering or stuff like that, but he'd give everything a go and we laughed a lot. He and John got on like a house on fire, the jokes went back and forth, day after day, and when it came to the end of the summer and it was time for him to go to college, I could tell that both of the lads were sorry to see him leave.

'Do you know what I'm going to tell you?' John asked him. We were sitting in the empty kitchen of a half-built house on the last day of the young fellow's last week working with us. 'I don't think I ever laughed as much as I did the past few weeks. We'll miss you when you're gone. I hope they appreciate you above in the university.'

The young fellow smiled.

'It's true,' Thomas said, and we all knew that if something moved Thomas to speak, then it must be true.

'Now, one last joke for the season. What's ET short for?'

'Extra Terrestrial?'

'No – because he has little legs.'

'What did the hobo have on his headstone?'

'I give up.'

'Here to stay.'

And the two of them were off again, spluttering and laughing.

Driving home that evening, I said: 'Wasn't it good to hear what the boys had to say?'

He nodded. When I told Miriam what they'd said, she just shrugged.

'Of course they'll appreciate him at the college. He has brains. Why wouldn't they appreciate him? What a silly thing to say.'

The day we headed for the university there was no question of hiring a car. We drove up in the van – me and him. Miriam found some reason to have to stay at home. She wouldn't go against his wishes, but neither would she want to be seen driving in the van with us. So the farewells were said at home, and we were waved off without too much fuss. I think it was a relief all round; I know it certainly was for me.

The van was well battered at that stage, but we did three or four laps of the university campus, just to let everyone see that the young fellow had good working-class credentials. I had no problem with that. He'd spent the summer earning his living by the sweat of his brow, so as far as I was concerned he was entitled to his hour of proletarian glory.

After we'd unloaded his bags and put them in the apartment – even then 'flats' were a thing of the past – we went and had something to eat.

'You'll enjoy it here,' I said.

'I think I will. I'm really looking forward to it.'

'That's good to hear. It'll be a lot freer than the boarding school.'

'That's for sure.'

And then something very strange happened. We had chatted all the way up to the city, but suddenly it was like a bulb had blown and we had nothing left to say. We finished our coffees, and I paid the bill and dropped him back to where he was staying. We shook hands. I slipped him an extra couple of bob, and before I was back in the van the apartment door was closed and I could see him framed in the window, laughing, talking earnestly with whomever else was there. In those few minutes it was like a lot of things had changed, like he'd stepped away from me and I had this awful, abandoned feeling that the gap might never be bridged again.

On the drive back home, and probably because of the way I was feeling, I found myself thinking of the journey home from Egypt for Miriam's father's funeral – the three of us squashed in the little car we had back then, but despite the knot in my stomach I'd had hope, I'd had happiness and I'd had a lot of dreams. But that night, coming down from the university, I remember thinking about how much things had changed between us all. It was like Miriam and I were drained and finished, like we'd run out of energy, out of life. I felt like I was a hundred years old. I had to remind myself that I was only 41 and Miriam was only 36. It felt like everything was gone. I was thinking about the Tremeloes song 'Me and My Life', but I didn't know if it was me or the young fellow who really wanted to be *away, away, away.*

When I drove into the yard, the house was in darkness. Then I remembered that it was a night-class evening, so I went straight to the workshop and lost myself in some piece of work or other. When Miriam got back she walked straight into the house, even though there were lights in the workshop, even though the house was pitch black, even though I'd just dropped her son to university.

And that's how it went from there on. The pair of us just rattled around the house, trying to avoid each other as much as we could. Miriam was working four days a week in her uncle's shop, and I worked every hour God sent, mostly to keep from having to be at home. In the evenings she had her night classes and her work at the Citizens' Centre and her trips to the pictures with her mother or Liz. I had my workshop. Everyone was satisfied and no one was happy.

In his second year in college, the young fellow began to get interested in politics. I wasn't impressed. My philosophy was that you keep your head down and your mouth shut and you get on with it. You don't draw attention to yourself, and you don't invite trouble into your life. And then he started bringing these fellows home at the weekends, fellows from the university. They were the kinds of guys who knew everything about everything, and whatever they didn't know about they'd pretend they did, spouting off about this, that and the other, full of bullshit and half-baked ideas. I never took to most of them.

They'd sit at our kitchen table and spew out rubbish about the world and what needed changing and what was waiting to be done and how they were the ones who'd work to make it happen. And I'd sit there and listen and think to myself that the sight of work of any kind would lead to the annihilation of half of them. I started thinking of them as the dodo brigade, extinction waiting to happen. I think it was their blind faith in their own half-cocked philosophies that really got to me.

They had no interest in listening, no practical ideas, no notion beyond a short-sighted and total conviction that their genius would see them through and that the rest of us mere mortals would breathe a sigh of relief once we recognised that brilliance. As pretentious a collection of arseholes as you're ever likely to meet.

Mostly, when we were honoured by their company, I'd have my bit to eat as fast as I could and then disappear out to the workshop. Sometimes, the young fellow would bring me a cup of coffee and we'd have a chat, and then I'd tell him to head back in to his friends.

'You're not mad about them,' he'd say.

And I'd shrug and smile and say: 'Ah, sure, you know yourself ...'.

And he'd laugh.

Sometimes Miriam would come out and give me a bollocking.

'What is it with you? Could you not even sit there until the meal was over? Could you not be civil enough to sit at the table until the meal is finished? Is that too much to ask? Why couldn't you just sit and listen? Are you afraid you might learn something? Are you afraid someone might teach you something, open your eyes a little, make you realise there's a world beyond this town? What am I saying, that there's a world beyond your workshop and your van and your building jobs and Tweedledum and Tweedledee for company till the day you die? There's even a world beyond Zip City, you know? Is that what you're afraid of, knowledge, new ideas, a challenge, having your preconceptions questioned?'

I'd say nothing because I didn't see any point in arguing. What was I to say – that despite all their paper brilliance in examinations they hadn't a decent idea between them? Was I to tell Miriam that the big words and fancy notions were as useful as a blunt jigsaw to a brain surgeon? She'd accuse me of not understanding or not wanting to understand. She'd tell me, as she had done in the past, that I was *a prisoner of technical ignorance*. It was a clever phrase because it had all kinds of connotations – my technical college *instruction* as opposed to the young fellow's university *education*; my technical *job* as opposed to his academic *career*. It was thought out, no doubt about it. I resisted the occasional urge to refer to her own foray into night-*schooling*, but from time to time I'd smile at the idea.

Sometimes, in the days after the dodos had left, I'd overhear Miriam talking to her mother or Liz or whoever happened to call to the house, singing their praises and throwing ridiculous assurances around the place that the young fellow and his comrades-in-harm would oversee a revolution in this country. I could hear the pride in her voice about how passionate he was in wanting things to change for the better.

Did I resent that? Maybe I did. Maybe, in my stupidity, I allowed myself to be reminded occasionally of how at one time there had been passion between the two of us, and then between the three of us, and how much of an outsider I now was, with all Miriam's passion still there, but all going into supporting issues and ideas and hare-brained possibilities.

Maybe I was jealous, but more than that I was worried. It wasn't really Miriam's ramblings that got to me, not below the surface level anyway. It was my fear of how committed the young fellow was. As the months rolled by, I could see the effect he was having on the others he was hanging around with, the dodos. They'd stopped talking so much and started listening to what he had to say. And the thing was, what he had to say sounded like it made a damn sight more sense than any of the twaddle they'd come up with. He was quoting Marx, the line about *the proletarians have nothing to lose but their chains* and that thing about *from each according to his ability, to each according to his need*. Not that I believed it. Every time I heard it I thought of the Gouger and every lazy fucker I'd ever worked with. There was a legion of handle-hangers and self-appointed architects stretching back across the years, the ideas-men you meet on every site and in every factory, the fellows whose main, even solitary, ambition is to avoid work.

But the young fellow wasn't just quoting Marx and Engels and the like, he was coming up with his own stuff too. He was always talking about commitment to the ideals he believed in. He didn't talk about *us* or *them* or *we*, it was about how *he* saw things, and fairly early on in the game I got the impression that he was about twelve steps ahead of the rest of them in his thinking. But then, that didn't surprise me either.

I remember one evening around the kitchen table; before I went back to the workshop, he was talking about rewards for the efforts we put in.

'People get repaid many times over, but it's not about the money.'

'People need money to live, they have that expectation,' one of the others said.

'My father,' he said, and he put his hand on my arm as he spoke, 'my father is a craftsman and he's a builder. I've seen him on site, doing work, getting paid the rate for the job. But I see the work he does in his workshop, the work that's precious to him, the care and time that goes into making a blanket box or a piece of furniture. The money he gets will never recompense him for that effort and the care and love that goes into that work. His reward is in the making, the creation, the delivery of something that he knows will be treasured long after he and you and I are gone. That's real wealth. Financial riches are a seduction, a deception. A revolution is not simply about changing a flag or a face on a postage stamp. It's about finding a way to mend broken hearts. Doesn't each of us want our treasure to be where our heart is?'

I could see that the others were listening, and they were impressed; they were taking him seriously. And that, as far as I was concerned, was the danger. The better he was at what he was doing – the more convincing he was to others – the greater the danger he might be to himself

But afterwards, in the workshop, I stood at the bench, looking out on the garden and the river and the deep blueness of the evening sky, and thinking about how wonderful it was that he knew what my work meant to me, that he understood what I was about. And I was thinking about the touch of his hand on my arm and that made me smile.

There was one of his friends that I did like. He was different from the rest. For a start, he wasn't in the university. And secondly, he was older than the others, closer to my own age. He'd been involved in the fishing business up on the lake, but the fishing was kaput at that stage.

The first time I saw this chap was one evening, here. I was in the workshop, and he stepped outside the back door of the house for a smoke. I could see him from where I was working. He was rambling around the van, reading the lettering on the side panels. When he finished his smoke, he stubbed out the butt, put it in a matchbox and put that into his jacket pocket. I liked that. Then he wandered across to the workshop and stood in the doorway, watching me work, and when he opened his mouth this traffic jam of words came out, one rear-ending the next.

'I cou ... cou ... cou ... cou ... could wo ... wo ... wo ... work for you as a te ... te ... te ... telephonist,' he said, miming a telephone in his hand. 'C ... C ... C ... C ... C ... A ... R Ltd. Th ... th ... thank you for ca ... ca ... ca ... ca ... calling.'

I just stood there with my mouth open, looking at this lunatic in the doorway, listening while he stammered his way through the company name. It must have taken him thirty seconds to get it out. And then he stopped, as though he were expecting an answer from me, a job offer, a partnership in the firm. I stared and he stared, and then a grin spread like a slow wave across his face and he pointed at me and laughed uproariously.

'I go ... go ... got you there.'

And that was Peter. He had no airs and graces. What you saw was who he was. He was decent man who'd been driven out of the fishing business because he couldn't make a living. I took to him that very first time we met. He had a down-to-earth feeling about him, and a decency that I recognised and admired. It's something I hope I have myself.

The second time he came down to stay for a weekend, he told me about this little fishing boat he had up on the lake. He said it was in too dangerous a state to take out, but that he'd had it since he was a teenager; it had been handed down to him by his father's uncle. We got talking, and I told him that if he provided the materials I'd fix it up for him, get it seaworthy again. He was all on for paying me for my time, but I was adamant that no money would change hands.

'If you pay me, I won't do the job,' I said. 'I've never spent time repairing a boat; it'll be a learning process for me – so, no money.'

I could see by him that on the one hand he wasn't convinced I could get it fit to use, but on the other he really wanted it back out on the water. We arranged that I'd drive up the following Monday and I'd spend the week working on it, and he'd come up on the Friday to see how things were going.

When I told Miriam about the plan, she was delighted. I think she thought I was gradually being sucked into dodo land, and that sooner rather than later I'd be converted to the brave new world. The truth was that I was looking forward to a week away on my own, but I said nothing.

Heart of Gold – Neil Young

*T*he week I spent up on the lake was one of the best weeks of my life. It was beautiful and peaceful up there. I got into a routine from the day I arrived. The boat was up on a small hill, a grassy hummock set back from the beach. It was a good place to work. Most of the time there was a soft, cool breeze coming off the lake, and there were a few trees that offered a shadow of shade during the midday heat.

I'd get up really early in the morning and set to working on the boat. I'd have five or six hours done before I hit the hottest part of the day. When that came I'd take a chair and my lunch and the newspaper and sit in the shade of the trees, just relax and have a bite to eat and read the paper. Some days I'd try my hand at the simple crossword, but I could never get even that finished. When the sun was at its highest, it would get that hot that even the birds would stop singing and there'd be this baking stillness. Nothing moving on land, maybe a boat out on the lake, but more often not even that. The blue sky, the big blinding splash that was the sun, the water reflecting the sky off its back, the few trees snapping and cracking above me – nothing else to see or hear.

Sometimes I'd doze off, and the singing of the birds as they came back to life would wake me and I'd look out over the water and take it all in before getting stuck into the job again, carrying on where I'd left off, putting in another couple of hours.

I'd finish work in the late afternoon, and got into the habit of walking right to the far end of the beach as a way of relaxing after the concentration of the day. It was even more beautiful down there on the point, water to the left hand, water to the right, and when I looked straight ahead nothing but water to the edge of the earth. I'd sit there sometimes and sing '(Sittin' on) The Dock of the Bay', not that Otis Redding and Steve

Cropper would necessarily have recognised my version, but I enjoyed it and the birds never complained.

On the way back, I'd have a wash in the lake and then put on clean jeans and a clean T-shirt and head down to the café in the village. It was about a mile from where I was working, but I never took the van. By the time I was making my way down, the sun was always sinking, the breeze was building off the water and it was pleasant to go rambling.

The café was called Renée's. The first evening I walked in I was the only customer in the place, and I got talking to the woman who worked there; she seemed to be cook, waitress and chief bottle-washer.

'You must be Renée,' I said.

'That's me.'

She had what I took to be an American accent, but it turned out to be Canadian.

'You didn't walk away?'

'Very droll,' she said.

'It was worth a try. Not everyone knows the song.'

'My mother was a big Four Tops fan. It was a hit the year I was born.'

'Sixty-eight.'

'Oops. Not everyone knows that either.'

'Could be worse,' I said. 'You could have been born the year it was originally released.'

'You telling me that it's not a Four Tops original?'

'I am. It was a hit for a group called The Left Banke – with an e at the end – in '66, written by two of the guys in the band for Renée Fladen-Kamm. She was the girlfriend of one of the band members.'

'I'm impressed.'

'Trivia,' I said. 'It's my stock in trade.'

'Well, I'm impressed.'

The following evening, Renée was smiling when I walked through the doorway.

'I called my Mom last night, told her about that band, The Left Banke, with an e at the end! She said to tell you the Four Tops will always be the defining version, but my guess is that she never heard of the other version or of the band. We had a giggle about it.'

'I'm glad I didn't cause a family feud.'

I didn't get to talk much to Renée that night. The place was busy, and she was on the go, non-stop. She waved when I was leaving and I waved back.

Outside, beyond the café lights, it was pitch black. I stood on the empty road, acclimatising myself to the darkness. Once I got my bearings from the stars, I was on my way. Rounding the bend, at the edge of the village, I could pick up the lesser darkness of the lake, and the stars swimming silently in its vast, flat water.

When I got back to the boat I sat on the end of the small pier that jutted into the waters of the lake, and listened to the slapping of the night waves against the stone below me. Beyond the lake there was a suggestion of a rising moon behind the hills, but I was too tired to wait and see it rise. Instead, I unrolled my sleeping bag and mat and bedded down in the back of the van, something I hadn't done in a long, long time.

And that became the pattern for the week – early morning work, a break in the midday heat, back to work for the afternoon, a walk along the beach, a wash in the lake, then a ramble down to the café. I was happy. The work was going well. It was interesting because I'd never done anything like that before. I'm the kind of fellow who gets seasick crossing a bridge on a windy day, so boats are foreign to me. But the more I worked on Peter's little vessel, the more I admired the craft that had already gone into it – probably thirty or forty years before – and the more I recognised *that*, the more I enjoyed what I was doing. This wasn't just a job, it was the continuation of a tradition, and though I'm no shipbuilder, I recognised that the man who had built that boat had made it to last and I was determined that the next person to work on it would know that I'd put the effort in too.

I worked late on the Thursday evening, worked until the last glow had been squeezed out of the sky, and even then I worked a bit longer by the beam of the van's headlights. Afterwards, I walked the beach in the dark and plunged into the black water of the lake, trying not to think of what might be out there in the murk. By the time I got to the café Renée was on the verge of closing, but she signalled me to come in.

'I thought you'd deserted me.'

'I was working late. The guy who owns the boat is due up tomorrow. I want to have it ready.'

'Shipshape?'

'Very punny.'

'So, how goes it?'

'Pretty well. Actually, I'm pleased with how it's gone.'

'When are you heading for the hills?'

'Saturday probably.'

She nodded and turned to prepare the food. I stood at the counter and we talked about the boat and about Peter. She didn't know him – he'd left the area before she'd arrived – but she knew the boat.

'So what took you all the way from Canada to here?'

'I thought it was love, but it turned out just to be sex. And then I discovered I liked this place, I mean this little village and this little building, and once the red-hot lover had decamped, I found I was really happy here, much happier than before he decamped.'

'I can understand that. It's a beautiful place – a good place to get lost.'

'Or to find.'

'That too.'

She busied herself with the food preparation. I picked a newspaper from a table and flicked through it. The world out there, beyond the lake, behind the hills, was still turning, apparently.

'Now!' she said, putting a plate and cutlery on the table. 'Bon appétit.'

'Will you join me?' I asked.

'Are you sure you want that? I won't be offended.'

'Yes, please do sit with me. I have more than enough of my own company.'

'Okay,' she said. She locked the café door and brought a mug of coffee and some olives from the kitchen.

We sat together in the light of the candles in their wax-studded wine bottles.

'Have you ever wondered about the purpose of birds?' Renée asked. 'I mean, apart from singing?'

'I haven't. But I will.'

'This morning I was out back, preparing some vegetables. I mean out back, back, in the yard behind the café. There were these four birds, they were flapping up then sliding down the sky. I wondered what their function was, whether they knew their own purpose.' She laughed and blushed. 'I need to get out more.'

'The birds that fly about have their nests.'

'Sorry?'

'Something I heard somewhere. Don't remember where, or even if that's the correct wording. Funny, it just popped into my head.'

'You're spending too much time with this lunatic,' she pointed to her head and crossed her eyes.

I ate my meal and she sipped her coffee. I felt more relaxed there than I'd felt in my own kitchen for several years. Something about the companionship of amiable strangers I suppose. Even the silence was different. It wasn't hanging there waiting to be broken. There were no expectations and no assumptions, just two people sharing a table, spending some time, not feeling pressurised and not feeling they had to tread carefully around each other.

'How long since you and your boyfriend … I'm assuming it was a man … went your separate ways?' I asked.

'It was a man – sort of,' she grinned. 'Two and a half years.'

'Do you mind if I ask something personal?'

'Shoot.'

'Do you miss any of it?'

'I miss the intimacy.'

I nodded.

'But I don't miss him, if that's your question.'

I nodded again.

'It's like, in my memory, the intimacy has nothing to do with him. The intimacy, the memory of it, is an emotion. He's just an asshole.'

She stood up.

'Would you like some coffee?'

'Yes please.'

'Would you like some of my all-American, momma's original recipe apple pie?'

'How can I refuse?'

She went into the kitchen and I followed, carrying my plate.

'You didn't have to do that.'

'It's okay. I'm domesticated.'

She poured two coffees and cut two slices from an enormous apple pie.

'We could sit out back, but the mosquitos love me. Is it okay if we stay here in the café?'

'Of course,' I said.

And so we did, and Renée told me about small-town Canada in the '80s. I said it sounded just like my home village.

'It's not the geography, is it? Not the number of streets or houses or population. It's the state of mind, and the creeping smallness of the state of mind. That's the bit that got to me. Even the biggest people there had tiny minds, closed like clams.'

I mentioned 'My Little Town', and she disappeared into the kitchen and came back with Paul Simon's *Still Crazy After All These Years* album and put it in the CD player.

'You were, what … 9 when that was released?'

'Blame it on my mom's influence again.'

'It's a great album.'

We listened while Simon flew his bike past the factory gates.

'After Saturday, what's next for you?' Renée asked when the track ended.

'Back home, back to the day-to-day stuff … back home.'

'You sound sad about going home.'

'Maybe I am.'

'Why?'

And then I started talking, and it was like I couldn't stop, and I told her about the evening in the workshop and Miriam's blue halter-neck dress and the half-open clasp.

'Were you obsessed about what it might be like to open it, the little snap it makes?'

'I suppose I was.'

'It's something we remember, isn't it? Women, I mean. The first time it happens.'

'Is it?'

'It is for me. I was 13.'

'Bloody hell, you were very young.'

'Too young,' she paused, remembering, and then she smiled. 'But there's something satisfying and reassuring about that moment of opening a clasp, when it's done easily, with just the one hand. That's a million miles from the teenage fumbling.'

'Yes, it is.'

'It's a strange thing, I've often thought, but more often than not, when a bra is unclasped, it stays in place. There's that other moment of waiting to see who'll take it off completely – him or her or neither.'

'Yes.'

'Did you think your wife might cry if you'd undone the clasp?'

'I hadn't thought about that. I just assumed she'd be mad at me. She's been mad at me for a long, long time. All the things that were there between us are gone, lost somewhere back along the road.'

'How can you be sure you've lost her?'

'I hear it in the way she doesn't talk to me,' I said. I had no idea where that thought had come from, but it was suddenly and blindingly clear, and I recognised the truth in it.

We sat for a long time, saying nothing. Renée picked at the candle wax on the wine bottle and I nursed my cup of coffee. Paul Simon sang the last few notes of 'Silent Eyes', and first one and then a second candle guttered out on the nearby tables.

'There go the profits,' I said.

Renée laughed quietly.

'I'd best be going, early starts for both of us,' I said.

She nodded.

'And thank you for listening.'

'I'm sorry you're leaving,' she said. 'I don't get too many conversations like this. Not too many evenings to sit and talk.'

'Me neither.'

She walked me to the door.

'I'll see you before you leave?'

'I certainly hope so.'

'Good.'

I saluted and set off across the empty square and into the darkness beyond, and then I stopped, remembering, and retraced my steps. The lights were still on in the café. Renée was setting tables for the morning. I tapped on the window. She looked up, smiled and crossed to open the door.

'Don't I know you?' she laughed.

'I just remembered,' I said. 'About the birds, what I heard. I just wanted to tell you. "Even the birds of the air have their nests." '

'That's beautiful. Who wrote it?'

'My son said it.'

'It's beautiful.'

We hesitated, she in the lighted doorway, me outside, and our shadows lay together on the sandy street, and then I saluted again and was gone into the night.

I worked hard right through Friday. I knew Peter would be driving up that afternoon, and I wanted everything to be done and dusted by the time he arrived. There's nothing I hate more than still being on the last legs of a job when it should be finished. It's always a disappointment to the customer, and it's always a disappointment to me. I was particularly determined that the boat would be seaworthy when he arrived. And it was.

Peter's old car came stuttering down the road in the late afternoon. It was the first time I'd noticed that he drove as he spoke, in fits and starts. The funny thing was that when he got out of the car he made a point of not looking at the boat or going near it. He stood there making small talk with me, asking how I'd enjoyed my week at the lake, telling me he'd seen the young fellow and how he'd sent his best wishes and wasn't it a peaceful spot? And I said yes, it was, and yes, it was easy to be happy with just the sun and the water, and yes, it would be a good place to live out the rest of a life. Finally, I pointed to the boat.

'You probably want to see how I've spent my time up here.'

We walked across the patch of grass and sand to where the boat was lodged in its harbour of blocks. I stood back and left him to the inspection. He walked around the boat several times, looking under and over. He climbed inside and disappeared into the wheelhouse and down into the galley. He was gone for quite a while. I felt I'd done a good job, but you never know if someone else's expectations are way above your own. Then he reappeared, climbed out over the side and circumnavigated the boat again. Finally, he walked slowly back across the grass, wordless, soundless, his hand outstretched. It was all I needed to see, that and the brightness of tears in his eyes.

When Peter did find the words, they were effusive. He was thrilled. It was like I'd given him a new boat. He had never dreamed I'd do what I did. He had expected a patch here and a board there, but nothing like the work I'd done. He hadn't dreamed it would be seaworthy. He couldn't believe how much I'd done, and he couldn't wait to take the boat out. In fact, he insisted that we take it out. So off we went, getting it up on the rollers, manhandling it down to the slip at the water's edge, easing it into the small, welcoming wavelets, getting the engine from the ramshackle shed across the lane, priming and cursing and priming and cursing until, at last, it throttled into life.

And then off we went, out onto the lake. And that was all fine and dandy till we got around the harbour wall and clear of its protection. Suddenly, it seemed there was a wind coming from the left and a wind coming from the right, and they seemed to be blowing together and separately by turns and chopping up the water like a lumberjack at the foot of a tree.

I could feel myself turn green. I could sense the blood drain from my head and feel the argument going on between my legs and my stomach all at the same time. Peter laughed and told me this was nothing. I told him in no uncertain terms that I'd never been out on a boat before. He told me to keep my eyes focused on one spot on the horizon. He promised it would get calmer once we got clear of the point and out on deeper water, and he was right. Once we moved away from the land, the chopping gave way to calm, clear water, smooth as a planed plank.

At last I allowed myself to look back in the direction from which we'd come. There was the point, and beyond it my van parked at the head of the beach, and a hundred yards away the wall where I'd sat at the close of every day. And there, standing on the end of the wall, was Renée. I waved, but just as I did she turned and started back along the wall, away from us.

When we reached the middle of the lake, Peter dropped the anchor and threw a handful of fishing lines over the side. A few minutes later he pulled in a couple of fish and gutted them before taking them down to the galley and frying them. When he called me down into the cramped space that could just about seat the pair of us there were fish and olives and bread and coffee on the small table.

'Eat, my fr … fr … friend,' he said. 'We will eat togeth … togeth … er.'

And we did, and we talked. I told him I was concerned about the young fellow, worried that he was getting in to the whole politics thing way over his head.

'He's a g … go … goo … good man.'

'I know that. It's just the others, the ones around him; they're the ones who bother me. Present company excluded, of course.'

'I wo … wo … wouldn't wo … wo … worry about him, he has his he … he … head screwed on. He'll be all right.'

'Thanks, thanks,' I said. 'I value your opinion.'

'And I'll tell you another th … th … thing,' Peter laughed: 'he's a damn sight be … be … better sailor than you are. He did … did … didn't inherit his sea legs from you!'

Little do you know, I thought. Little do you know.

We finished our food, washed the few dishes and went back up on deck to find a round, fat moon rising out of the hills on the opposite side of the lake, and suddenly we were just these two silver men in a silver boat, floating on a silver lake, under a big silver sky. I stayed at the top of the steps gawking, lost in the beauty of it all.

After a while, Peter walked to the prow of the boat and stood there, outlined against the shining sky, and he began to sing in this deep, beautiful bass voice. He sang 'Blue Moon'. He sang it as if the lake were his stadium and the stars were his audience, sang it through, word perfect, note perfect. And when he'd finished he remained where he was for a moment, a statue against the sky, and then he turned and smiled this rueful smile: 'See, not a si … si … sign of a st … st … st … stammer.'

We must have been out there for hours, watching the moon and her sister glide across the sky and the lake. It was well after midnight when we hauled in the anchor, started up the grumbling engine and headed back to the harbour.

I had a good night's sleep, then shared a breakfast of bread, fish and coffee with Peter. I packed my stuff into the van and listened as he told me, for the umpteenth time, how grateful he was and what a job I'd done.

I was happy just to see him happy. He was all on for having me stay, but I could see that what he really needed was to be out on the water, enjoying again the pleasure so long denied him, and my being with him would only hold him back.

'The waves are waiting,' I said. 'If I had a new lathe I'd want to be in my workshop and using it, not trying to teach someone else how to do it. I've had a brilliant time here and now it's your turn. I hope the winds are always kind to you.'

He shook my hand, thanked me again and reminded me not to be worrying about the young fellow, and then I walked down to the harbour wall with him, helped him to cast off and stood watching the boat move out onto the brightening waters of the lake, where Peter could test himself again. I could see how he loved the lake, or the sea as he called it, and I wasn't going to be in his way.

Only when I'd done a final check that I hadn't forgotten anything and that I was right for the road did I see the neatly folded note tucked under the windscreen wiper. I opened it and read the copperplate message.

Hope your voyage was a good one. Sorry I missed you. Maybe I'll see you tomorrow night if you're still about. If not, it was good meeting you. R.

I thought my heart had stopped – a feeling I hadn't had in a long, long time. I found myself delighted that Renée had come up to the harbour, and sorry she hadn't been there in time to join us on our trip the evening before. I was sure that Peter would have enjoyed her company. I was happy, too, that she'd left that message, and excited at the prospect of seeing her again. I reread the note, put it in the glove compartment and swung the van around, driving slowly down the narrow road that led to the village, eager to be there, but savouring the journey.

I hadn't been in the square so early before, and, quiet as it was in the evening time, it was like a deserted village now. Not a sinner moving, one sleeping cat on a windowsill, two trucks outside the shad-owed open door of a garage, the occasional sound of a hammer on metal.

The café seemed empty, but when the bell dinged on the door Renée stepped out of the kitchen, a smile catching fire as she did.

'I'm so glad to see you.'

'And I'm glad to see you. I'm sorry we missed each other last night. I could see you from the boat, but we were too far out to come back. I only found your note this morning.'

'That's okay. The boat didn't sink then? You must have done a good job.'

'No, it didn't sink.'

We sat and talked. I drank some coffee. Renée made me some food for the journey, and wouldn't take any money when I tried to pay her. She said I'd been her best customer in years.

'And now you go back to your life.'

'This is my life too,' I said.

'Of course, but your real life, your daily life … you know what I mean.'

'I know what you mean.'

'Well, if you ever find yourself back in these parts, don't be a stranger. And there's always a spare room.' She handed me her card. 'It really has been lovely spending time with you, Joseph. It's been wonderful.'

'Yes, it has been a great time and brilliant to meet you,' I said.

We sat together in silence, comfortable yet uncertain.

'I can think of so much else to say, but it may not be the time,' Renée smiled.

I nodded, and then I said: 'I felt he'd found my letters and read each one out loud.'

' "Killing Me Softly"…'.

'You know your music.'

'I'm just the apprentice,' she said.

There was another silence before she reached across the table and laid her hand on mine, her small, dark hand on my big, bruised hand, and I found the courage to look her in the eyes. And then the doorbell jingled again and two men, who looked, by the cut of their overalls, as though they might have been working in the garage up the street, came in, laughing and talking loudly.

'The usual breakfasts and two strong coffees, Renée,' one of them said.

'Be right with you,' she said back as they thudded down into a booth. I wished I had more time, to tell her about Jacob's Ladder, about my life, about my unspeaking heart that seemed just to tick along because it had forgotten until that morning the differing rhythms that joy, anticipation and love can introduce into a beat.

'I'd better go,' I said. 'I have your card, your number. Will I give you mine?'

She shook her head.

'You'll only ring if and when you've thought things through. I might well ring out of madness.' She grinned a crooked grin.

'And that would be okay.'

'It could be, but who knows? Anyway, you have my number.'

She walked me to the door. As we passed the two men in the greasy overalls she said: 'Be with you in a moment, boys.'

'No hurry,' one of them said. 'No hurry.'

Afterwards, on the long drive home and in the days and weeks that followed, I thought about that man in the café, the man in the overalls, waiting for his breakfast, and recognised that there was something in the tone of his voice, in the way in which he repeated the words 'No hurry' that signalled his recognition, even as an outsider, of the importance of the moment. He knew Renée, knew her well enough to recognise that her walking me to the door and her not taking his order immediately, as she probably had done for months and months, was of importance, and he would not intrude into this part of her life. He and his companion had stepped back, as clearly as if they'd stepped outside the door, and left us to our silence and our conversation. And, I thought, if he could sense the tension between Renée and me then it must be real.

I kept her number, put her card in my workbook and, at the year's end, filed that journal as I've done all the others across the decades of my working life. There's not a job I've done or a contact I've made or a customer I've worked with whose details are not in one or other of those diaries. And Renée's number is there among them. I could find it in a moment if I wanted to.

There were no complaints from Miriam about my having been away this time. She was full of questions about the boat, but they were simply the opening gambit in a conversation aimed at uncovering whether Peter had succeeded in converting me into a true believer or not. I didn't compound her disappointment by telling her he hadn't even tried.

Have You Seen Her? – Chi-Lites

*E*ighteen months later, the young fellow qualified as a teacher and got a job in the city. On the day of his graduation, we took Miriam's car. It made sense, she said, because her mother was travelling with us. I didn't argue.

After the ceremony was over, the photographs had been taken and we'd met his friends and their parents, the four of us went for a meal. The restaurant we chose had a wedding breakfast going on in a room at the back, and I could see, right from the word go, that this irked Miriam. There was a lot of sighing, and when she spoke she spoke more loudly than was necessary, as though the laughter from the other room was a bother. And she kept asking her mother if she was all right.

'We should have booked somewhere quieter,' Miriam said.

'It's fine; the food is good here,' the young fellow said.

I could see that she still wasn't happy.

'Funny, isn't it?' I said to him. 'You went to boarding school in this city and you went to university in this city and now you'll be teaching in this city. All your education stuff has been here.'

'How can you call it *stuff*?' Miriam said sharply. 'Education is not *stuff*. Vans are *stuff*, furniture is *stuff*, kitchen units are *stuff* – education is not *stuff*. And of course he'll be teaching here; it's where the opportunities are, where life is, where things happen and where the people who matter are. You didn't expect that he'd come back and teach in the Tech at home, did you?'

'No,' I said. 'It was just an observation.'

I could see that the young fellow was upset by her outburst. He knew I'd only been passing a comment. We read our menus, and there was a silence that would deafen a bothered elephant.

'We should order some decent wine to go with the meal,' Miriam said. 'This is a big day, an important day. The house wine is probably watered down for that wedding thingy in there.'

'Mother,' the young fellow said, half-joking, wholly in earnest, 'it's not important at the moment, it really isn't.' She looked at him and I thought she was going to say something, but he smiled and laid his hand on her hand and said, very quietly: 'Now is not the time and this is not the place to let something like that upset you. It really isn't important.'

And that was that. I could see why people listened to him. Why, when he spoke, it was as if the final words had been spoken. That was more frightening than I was prepared to admit – not for me, but for him.

By the following summer he was getting more and more involved in politics. He started popping up in the audiences of those TV discussion programmes, asking questions, pushing the politicians to answer him. And the next thing we knew he was on the panels of speakers on these programmes. People were stopping Miriam or me on the street, saying things like: 'Oh, I saw your son on TV last night, he was great, talked a lot of sense. Pity there's not more like him.' I'd say nothing, just nod. But, if they said it to Miriam, she'd be in seventh heaven, as proud as punch, and she'd say: 'Yes, he was good, wasn't he?'

Around that time, his photograph began to appear in a couple of the papers, and then there were articles about him, and people would say to her: 'Oh he's going places. He's definitely on the up and up.' She'd smile and say: 'He is, he's doing well for himself. He has the brains for it.' And then there were articles by him, and the same people would say: 'That was a brilliant article your young lad had in the paper. I didn't understand all of it, but then I'm not a scholar. But the photograph was lovely. He's a handsome young fellow.' And she'd smile and say quietly: 'There's a lot of depth in what he thinks and writes.' And they'd say, 'Now you're talking.'

As for myself, I was wishing he'd keep his head down and his mouth shut and stay well out of the spotlight. I was old enough to know the kind of vicious people who were running this country back then, and smart enough to know that a keen brain, a bright mind and a loud voice might lead him into more trouble than reward. On the odd time I saw him I never said anything about it to him, and I certainly wouldn't say it to his mother.

By the time he'd been teaching for three years, we're talking about the summer of 2001, he was right in the thick of it. He was travelling around the country, giving talks, addressing meetings, organising rallies and all that kind of thing. I kept well out of it. I did what I was good at doing and got on with working and keeping my head down.

The country was like dry brush at that time, and had been for the guts of a year, just waiting for someone to toss a match into it. Sometimes Miriam would head off and spend two or three days with him and his 'associates' – her word, not mine. To me, for the most part, they were still just the same ragbag of malcontents and halfwits, the dodos. I wished the young fellow would come and visit more often. I imagined myself dissuading him from what he was doing. I'd be in the workshop of an evening and I'd be running all these emotional speeches and arguments through my head and imagining him nodding and saying: 'Yes, I take your point. You're right.'

But, then, the other part of me was glad that I didn't have to listen to the bullshit that his friends still went on with around the kitchen table when they did come to visit. And I knew, in my heart, that I probably wouldn't get the chance to talk to him on his own, and if I did I wouldn't have the courage to say anything. If I managed to stumble out a few words, he wouldn't be convinced by my argument anyway.

When Miriam did spend time travelling with him, she'd come back and either barge straight into the workshop and give me every detail or I'd have to wring whatever few bits and pieces of information I could out of her in the days that followed. Inevitably, the conversation would end with her saying: 'I know you're only asking out of duty. You don't really care.'

At the time I was never sure how far back or how deep that comment stretched, but it wasn't too long before I found out.

As that summer wore on, Miriam would be gone almost every weekend, and then it got to a point where she'd be gone for a week or ten days and I'd never know when to expect her back. I'd read in the newspaper about where the young fellow was and what he was saying, and I'd have some notion from what I read as to where she might be. And then, one morning at the end of that September, I woke up and the realisation hit me, out of nowhere, that she was gone and that she wouldn't be coming back.

I remember looking in her wardrobe and her cupboards and realising that there was very little left in any of them. For weeks she'd been taking stuff away when she left, but I'd presumed she'd brought it back for washing when she returned. Not so.

That morning I sat at the table eating my breakfast, and I thought back to the last time we'd spoken. It was in the workshop. An argument had started, and, like most of the arguments in those last few months, it was about the fact that I spent most of my time at work – out on jobs or in the workshop.

'You're like a block of your bloody wood,' she'd said. 'Look at yourself, Joseph, work is everything to you. You spend your days with it, you sleep with it, you drive it around in that bloody van and play music to it.'

Then she stopped for a moment. It was late in the evening, the sun was going down and there was this light coming through the workshop door behind her, this low, blinding light, and I couldn't see her face, but I could tell how upset she was by the shiver in her voice.

'There was a time when you felt so passionate about me that you hit my father and took me to another country,' she'd said. Her voice had been really quiet, and then she'd turned and left and I'd watched her walking down the garden and I'd thought how sexy she looked and how beautiful and how alone, but I was frozen into whatever I'd become. And I lost her.

That was three or four days before she left, and two weeks later it dawned on me that she wasn't coming back, and I had no idea what to do. And then I did what I always do when I don't know what to do – I got back to work.

To be honest, it was much the same routine as I'd had for years. I'd get up in the morning, grab something to eat, go to work, come home in the evening, make an evening meal, take a cup of coffee to the workshop, have a read of the paper and then get on with whatever was the job in hand.

Every now and then I'd see or read something about the young fellow in the paper and I'd think I really should catch up with him, but I'd put it off for as long as I possibly could, tell myself I'd do it next week or next month, and a year slid by in that way.

One evening the following October, I opened the paper and I saw that he was speaking at a rally in a one-horse town about sixty miles from here, so I made up my mind to get off my backside and go and see him.

I drove up the morning of the meeting and got there nice and early, a couple of hours before the rally was due to begin. I parked the van on the edge of the town square and found a coffee shop with chairs and tables outside, and that's where I planted myself. While I was sitting there eating, the other side of the square was a hive of activity. A trailer had been brought into the square to act as a platform, and there were fellows putting up loudspeakers, testing microphones, hanging banners and posters and testing the PA, and on and on it went. Then, from about eleven onwards, the square began to fill, the people came in their hundreds, pouring in from every street and alley. In a matter of twenty minutes the place was full.

The public meeting began at midday. There was speaker after speaker after speaker, all of them saying the same thing and all of them going on for way too long. And then the young fellow was talking. There was heckling and jeering and cheering, questions and answers, and to be fair he didn't talk for too long. Not surprisingly, what he had to say made more sense than anything that had come before. And then, as suddenly as it had started, the meeting was over and the world hadn't stopped turning and the government hadn't changed and the crowds began to drift away until, eventually, there were only two other people left in the square – him and this young woman.

I was sitting there, watching the two of them, and I could see that she was a really good-looking young one and I was thinking – if it comes to a toss-up between sex and politics, sex will almost always win, and I was smiling at the thought. And all the time she was talking away, nineteen to the dozen, and he was standing there with this piece of stick in his hand and he was drawing or writing or doodling in the sand. When I looked more closely at the young woman I could see that she was wearing this pair of FMBs and she had a skirt that was more like a belt and a bright red blouse with a seriously plunging neckline. And for some reason this poem that I'd learned in primary school came into my head:

Into the valley of Death
Rode the six hundred.

And the closer I looked the more I realised she really wasn't his type. She was still talking to him, and then she was gone, slipping away down an alley at the side of the square.

The young fellow went on drawing in the sand, until something caught his attention, because he looked up and a second later he saw my van and then he saw me. He scrabbled out whatever it was he was drawing or writing and headed across the square, and I got up and rambled over to meet him.

'Were you drawing plans for the house?' I asked.

That big, crooked grin spread across his face and he laughed and shook my hand, and we went back and sat outside the coffee shop and I bought us some food and we talked. What did we talk about? We talked about football. And the weather. And work. Bullshit stuff of no consequence. He told me that Miriam was in a town about fifty miles up the road and he was sure she'd be sorry she'd missed me, and I mustered whatever sincerity I could and said I was sorry I'd missed her too. And suddenly we had nothing more to say. We just sat there and tried to pretend we were eating, and then he looked at his watch and I took the hint and said I'd better be going, that I had a job to price. We shook hands and wished each other well, and he went one way across the square and I went the other. When I got to the van I opened the door and then I turned and watched him walking away; the parting glimpse I caught of him that day was as he rounded the side of the platform and disappeared down an alleyway. And all the way home I thought about the great things I'd promised to say when I got the chance, and I thought about the silence between us.

The last time I talked to the young fellow was about three weeks before it happened. It was a spring evening and I was in the workshop when I saw a car pulling up on the street, and he got out and came in through the gateway. The car drove away. I thought for a second that it might have been Miriam driving, but I couldn't be sure. It was there and then it was gone.

He came into the workshop and we shook hands and then he sat on the bench inside the door. He asked what I was doing and I showed him this inlaid blanket box I was making for a couple who were expecting their first baby. He said it was a beautiful piece of work, and then I put it away. We went inside to the kitchen and I made some coffee, found a couple of cakes in a tin and brought them back outside.

'It's warmer in the workshop,' I said. 'That's where I spend most of my time.'

I have a little stove in the corner for winter time and chilly evenings in spring and autumn. The offcuts keep it going. I threw a handful in and we pulled the bench across and sat there, drinking our coffee, eating the cakes and talking and laughing. But this time it was totally different from the day in the Square after the meeting. This time we really talked, about the things that truly mattered.

I asked him how Peter was, and he said that Peter was doing fine. I asked how things were in his life. He smiled, the crooked grin, and said they were tough days we were living through, but he felt he was making progress, that people were listening. And then I told him I was worried about him.

'The thing that worries me is that when times get really tough, to put it bluntly, if and when the shit hits the fan and they come looking for you, will all these wide boys and university people just disappear, desert you? So-called friends have a habit of doing that, leaving you on your own. I know that from experience.'

'I'll never be on my own,' he said, and the smile crept crookedly across his face again. 'The poor are always with us.'

I couldn't disagree with that. And then we just sat there, two men sitting in the weak spring rays, a small fire warming them, content in their silence, and the sun went down and darkness crept in and lay at our feet. And then a car horn beeped on the street outside. We both knew it was for him, but we ignored it. It beeped again, longer this time, more persistent, and the young fellow got up to go and, just as he was passing, he put his hand on my shoulder and squeezed it, and then he was gone.

I stood up to follow him, but by the time I got to the gable of the house he was opening the car door. The light came on inside and I saw that it was Miriam who was driving. I raised my hand and waved, and she lifted her finger from the wheel in acknowledgement, and then they were gone.

The Spirit is Willing – Peter Straker and the Hands of Dr Teleny

*I*t was the Wednesday after it happened. I'd got in from work, grabbed a bite to eat, taken my cup of coffee out to the workshop and was standing there at the workbench leafing through the paper when I saw these three pictures of three young guys on the top of a page. There was the young fellow and two other chaps. Not a lot unusual in that. And then I started to read the story underneath, and on the third or fourth line down it said that the three of them had been executed the previous Friday.

I couldn't believe what I was reading. I just stood there, staring at the three faces, rereading the names and thinking it had to be wrong, that there must be some mistake, the wrong faces with the wrong story or something like that. It happens. Not everything you read in the paper is true, I know that. But the more I read the article, the more I realised there was no mistake. The names, the ages, the faces, everything fitted. And then I knew I was going to be sick and I just about made it to the back door before everything I'd eaten in the previous two days came up. How do I explain it? It was like I'd walked into a sauna in a fur coat – perspiration was dripping from me. In a matter of seconds my shirt and jeans were soaking and I was finding it hard to breathe. I leaned against the wall of the workshop, searching for a breeze, a drift of cool air, and then I sat on my hunkers, back against the wall, thinking I was going to faint, but the nausea passed, and eventually I could stand up.

I turned to go back inside, and as suddenly as it had gone the vomiting was back. But this time there was nothing but bile, green and black, like the insides of some rotting animal. And then that passed. Finally I had enough strength to get into the house, climb the stairs, take off my clothes and step into the shower and just stand there, letting the water drive the sweat from my skin. It couldn't reach the shock, hurt and despair inside. Afterwards I dressed in clean, dry clothes, but by the time I'd come back downstairs these were stuck to me too.

That's when the anger took over. The young fellow had been dead for five days and no one had bothered to contact me. No one had thought it worth their while to lift a fucking phone and ring me to tell me that my son was dead. Not a message, not a text, nothing. Just silence until I'd stumbled on the story in the paper.

I picked up the phone and rang Miriam's mobile number and it rang and rang and rang, and then I texted her and rang her and texted her and rang her, and I just kept getting the fucking answering machine. I sat at the kitchen table and dialled every five minutes and texted three or four times between every call, but nothing came back.

Then I thought – Liz! Liz will know what's going on. So I grabbed the paper from the workshop, jumped in the van and drove like a lunatic to her place. I remember storming in the door, slapping the paper on the table and shouting: 'What the fuck is this? Why didn't you tell me?'

She looked at the photographs, read the article. She knew nothing about the story either.

I stood there and watched the blood drain from her face, watched her crumple and cry, found myself with my arms about her shoulders, trying to comfort her.

When I got back home I spread the newspaper on the workbench and stared at the young fellow's photograph, wishing it alive. Then I tried ringing and texting Miriam again and again, all through that night and the following day and the one after that.

For three days I ate nothing, spoke to no one, did nothing but sit and wait for the phone to ring, for someone to explain. Then, on the fourth day, I did what I always do when I don't know what to do: I went back to work. I got up that morning, showered and went into the workshop. I took the newspaper from the workbench where it had lain since I'd come back from Liz's house, scrunched it into a ball and tossed it out into the yard, where I'd vomited on the gravel.

That afternoon I walked down to the town to get some bread and milk, and the same people who had stopped Miriam to tell her how wonderful it was seeing the young fellow on TV were now stopping me to sympathise.

'So, so sorry for your troubles.'

'He was a lovely young man; you must be devastated.'

'Really sorry to hear about your son.'

'A fierce tragedy, no one should have to bury a child.'

And I couldn't even tell them I hadn't known he was dead. I couldn't tell them that I'd found out the same way they'd found out, by reading a five-day-old story in a newspaper. I couldn't tell them that no one had thought it worthwhile to let me know, neither his friends nor his mother. I just couldn't tell them.

One man called to the house to sympathise. The Gouger. It turned out he was teaching in Zip City and had seen the story in the paper, like the rest. He drove out to see me, and sat in his car for an hour until I got home from work. He didn't trot out all the chestnuts that I'd been hearing on the street. He just said that he was really, really sorry and that he hoped I'd be okay, and then he spoke the truest words anyone had spoken.

'There's nothing I can say that'll make the slightest difference. I know that, but I wanted to try … in spite of the pointlessness.'

I tried to get back into my routine over the following months, and it was always the same – get up early, grab something to eat, work all day on a job, home for a bite in the evening, read through the paper while I had my coffee in the workshop, do a few hours there and then off to sleep. Every now and again I'd think that I should be doing something, trying to find out something, piecing things together, but then I'd put it off until another time.

It must have been seven months after the young fellow's death when I got home one evening and there was a letter on the mat in the hall. It was from Peter. Turned out he was in prison. I have the letter stored away somewhere, but I can't lay my hands on it just now. Anyway, the gist of it was that after the executions the crowd had scattered in every direction. Surprise, surprise, I thought. Peter went back up to the lake and tried to make a living at the fishing again, but the fishing industry was fucked. And then he started running what he called *odds and ends* across the lake, and then he got caught and ended up in the slammer. I knew by the fact that he didn't say what he'd been running that it must have been serious enough. In one bit of the letter, near the end, he wrote: *I never realised you could be so far from home so close to home, but that's what it feels like in here.*

I remember thinking: I must go and visit Peter in the prison. He's a good man; I'll go and see him, bring him up a few things. But I put that on the long finger as well, and about two months after his letter came I opened the paper one evening and read that he'd been executed too.

Something snapped in me that evening, and I picked up the phone and rang the hospital where I knew the young fellow's body had been taken after the execution. I got talking to this young woman doctor; she sounded like she was genuine, but she was far too cautious for me, and I could understand her uneasiness. The phones were often bugged, and no one knew who was listening in on whom or when. I gave her the name and I gave her the date and I asked her if there was anything she could do, any little bit of information she could get me, anything at all – I'd be grateful. She took my name and address and said that she'd see what could be done, but I remember hanging up from the call and thinking: that's the last I'll ever hear from you, sunshine.

Ten days later I got home to find a letter waiting for me. No name, no address, nothing – just a sheet of paper – and the minute I glanced at it I realised I was reading a post-mortem report. I was in the yard reading it, walking up and down and up and down, trying to keep from vomiting again. It was all there. Arrest. Detention. Questioning. Torture. Execution. I remember thinking how cold it was, the way the bastards systematically tortured and beat him and then crucified him.

When I read that report, a couple of things happened. The first was that I realised I wasn't reading about someone else's son, about the son of some feathery character who had appeared in the doorway of someone's mother's kitchen. As far as I was concerned, I was reading about my son. The second was that I realised I didn't want to live in a country where people were pulled off the streets, questioned, tortured and executed. I didn't want to be living in a country where we hadn't got beyond cruci-fying people. The report in the newspaper had said the three men were shot, but I was reading a post-mortem on someone who'd been crucified. And I didn't want to live in a country where my wife couldn't even lift the phone and tell me that our son was dead.

The following night I rang Ammar, my old friend in Egypt, and asked him if there was any chance of a start over there. And he said yes, there was plenty of work.

'You come right back here, Joseph. You still have the beard?'

'I still have the beard, Ammar.'

'Good man, good man. Yes, you come on back and I'll find you a place to live. You can stay with us while you're getting settled. The children have all grown up and gone. Rania will be pleased to have any company other than mine. It'll be just like old times, Joseph, just like the old days.'

I didn't contradict him. I just said I'd that finish things up here and then I'd be on my way.

I stopped taking on new work, updated my passport, made enquiries about letting the house, and then thought better of it and decided to lock it up instead. Liz said she'd keep an eye on it for me. I told Thomas and John they could use the workshop as a base and keep the business going for as long as they wanted. And that was about that.

I Can See Clearly
Now – Johnny Nash

The night before I was due to leave I was out in the workshop, checking that everything was in order for Thomas and John, taking one last look around, remembering how I'd fallen in love with that shed when I first saw it.

There's a song that Eddi Reader sings and she says something like, I wish we could live in photographs. I was thinking along those lines, about all the times I'd laughed in the workshop, the evenings when Miriam and the little fellow had come out to talk to me, the endless cups of coffee I'd carried or had carried to me across the yard outside, about the times the sun had shone in there on us, about each of those days and all that time and how it had disappeared like the brightest star, like a meteor streaking across the sky, ablaze then gone.

Anyway, I was just standing there, taking one last look around, mind wandering, when I saw this car pull up at the gate and these two young fellows got out; one of them, the driver, was about 19 and the other a year or two younger. They must have seen me through the window because they came right up the workshop and stood there in the doorway, neither in nor out. I knew the older chap's father. I'd worked with him on a few jobs, a damn good plumber.

I don't know if you've ever seen someone who's in shock, I mean real shock. They don't go pale or white, they go green. That's how these two young fellows looked: their skin was green, and not just their faces; their arms and hands were a faded shade of green.

I brought them into the workshop and sat them down on the bench. I made them tea, sweet tea with lots of sugar, and I made them drink it. And they kept glancing at each other, nodding at me when they thought I wasn't looking. The older fellow couldn't stop shaking. He'd drink a mouthful of tea and then he'd scrunch up this baseball cap he was carrying. One of them kept looking at the other, like each was waiting for the other to talk. Eventually the older guy did start talking. He just put down his mug and took a deep, deep breath.

'I know what I'm going to tell you is going to sound mad, boss, but I have to say it anyway.'

He looked at his colleague, but the younger guy had nothing to say. He just shrugged and stared at his feet.

'Today, after the dinner hour, we were driving, me and him,' he nodded to his companion. 'We were driving out of Emmaus and there was this chap hitching at the side of the road, so we stopped and he sat into the back seat and we drove on. And we were chatting away about things, football and the weather and ... just rubbish talk. And then he asked us where we were from, and we said here, and he laughed and said: 'That's where I'm from too.' And something about the way he said it or something in his accent made me look in the rear-view mirror, and the minute I did I recognised him ...'.

He paused and looked at his friend again, but the younger fellow just kept his head down and the older chap glanced over at me and then looked away, and his eyes followed a moth as it went swirling up into the rusty metal rafters then plunged back to the heat of the light.

'Look, I know what you're thinking, boss. You're thinking that I'm drunk or off my head or just crazy, and I know that your son died a year or more ago, but I remember him from when I was a kid, and I seen his picture in the paper and it was him. It was him. I swear. It was your son in the back of the car.'

The quiet one looked up, his eyes held mine and he nodded.

'I drove as fast as I could to the next petrol station and I pulled in, and the two of us leapt out and went and got some strong coffee, and when we come back out to the car he was gone. But I swear, I swear on my mother's life ... I swear on my own life ... it was your son in the back of the car. And we said we better come and tell you, and that's what we done.'

I stood there watching these two young boys, one without a word to throw to a dog and one who couldn't shut up, and I believed them. This wasn't like some fairy story about a feathery angel standing in a mist in the doorway of Miriam's mother's kitchen. This young fellow's words sounded true as a spirit level.

That night, after the young fellows had left, I rang Ammar and told him there'd been a change of plan. All bets were off.

Hold Your Head Up – Argent

*I*often think about those two young fellows and how they got here just in the nick of time. Another day and I'd have been gone. I know that if I talked to people about it they'd have theories, and all the predictable words would trip out – fate, coincidence, destiny, providence – and each would have a story from their own past to prove their point. Another good reason to keep my mouth shut. And anyway, the two young fellows brought me something more important than all the theories in the world: they brought me hope.

Every time I sit into the van, I turn on the engine and tune the radio till I find the kind of music I want, and then I start driving. And I'm always searching. Sometimes I see things I'd rather not see, but that doesn't stop me searching and it doesn't, for even a moment, stop me hoping.

One time I saw a woman and her child at a traffic light, waiting to cross the street, and something about the sight of that child made me wince. There was such pain in his eyes, this small boy standing on a street corner with his mother and his whole life story was already scratched in his face.

Another time I was standing on a railway platform, waiting for the trains from the east. I had an hour to kill before I could start on a job in a restaurant, and I drove down to the railway station, parked the van and stood in the shadow of an awning, watching the people come and go. Three trains left for the city and three trains came from the city, a rush to board, a rush to disembark, but two of us remained on the platform, a well-dressed man in his late 40s and me. I wondered if he, too, was waiting for someone. Waiting and hoping.

And then I heard the grumble of the early express train, and the grumble became a growl and then a roar, and it emerged from the haze of the long day's heat, its windscreen two burning eyes in the evening sun, thundering towards us at eighty miles an hour, all noise and power, its force sending tremors through the concrete beneath our feet. Just as it reached us, the man stepped off the platform and it caught him in mid-air and took him with it, as though he were just another passenger, and, in that moment, my breath went with him.

But, still, I keep looking. I could be driving through a town and I'll be watching the people walking the paths, scanning their faces all the time. Or I could be in the city, driving really slowly and I'll be looking down the alleys and the side streets, keeping an eye out for him. Or I might be stopped at traffic lights and I'll be looking in the windows of coffee shops because even there, even from the back, I'd recognise the shape of his head. Or I could be driving along at night, out in the middle of nowhere, and suddenly someone will appear out of the darkness, walking, and I'll slow down and watch them, watch them till they pass, just because, just in case.

And I know, when I do find him, the first thing I'll do is put my arms around him and give him the biggest hug anyone has ever got, because I haven't hugged him since he was 11 or 12. And then I'll hold him out at arm's length and look into his eyes and say: 'I love you, son. I love you.' And I'll never have loved him more than then.

Epilogue

What came first, the urge or the circumstance? I wonder about that now. Did the memory just become stronger and stronger, demanding to be told? Or did the circumstance resurrect the memory? I should have asked, but the thought didn't cross my mind that evening when the telephone rang and I heard her voice but had no idea who she was, not until she told me. Nor, I suppose, did she know mine. She spoke my name, it was a question, and I said: 'Yes, this is Joe.'

But I could hear the smile in her voice as she repeated my name: 'Joe'.

And then there was just that dead air that comes with silence on a telephone line. And she spoke my name again and then she said: 'You don't know who this is, do you?'

'No,' I said, 'I'm sorry, I don't.'

'Why should you? It's been such a long, long time.'

Then that silence again, that quietness that makes me think of all the birds on all the wires that loop and link across the hundreds or thousands of miles between one person and another, all those birds swinging and swaying or sitting perfectly still on telephone wires. And then the sound of that voice on the line.

'I'm sorry, it's strange to talk again after all this time. This is Ruth.'

'Ruth! My God, how long has it been? No don't tell me. Thirty-eight years.'

'I'm afraid so.'

'How are you? Where are you?'

'I'm living in France, Joe, have been since the late '70s. I'm more French than anything at this stage, I suppose.'

'I can't believe I'm talking to you,' I said, and I couldn't. It was like this was all happening in my head. 'How the hell did you find my number?'

'It's a long story. It started last year with a TV documentary about the troubles back home, about the disappeared and the dead. One of the names caught my attention and I wondered. Then I made some enquiries through the embassy here, and when I found the names and address of the young man's parents I wondered if it were you. So I got this number. I'm so, so sorry. I know I'm ten years late, but I'm really sorry.'

'Thank you. Thank you.'

That silence again, the birds on the bows of wire, one crow on a pole somewhere in the east of France, where it meets Belgium. That's what I was seeing in my head. One solitary, black bird on a post on the edge of one of those long-dead battlefields we read about in school.

'You're in the same business, more or less. I'll bet you're doing well.'

I laughed. 'I'm doing okay, Ruth. What about you? Are you married? Children? Still translating?'

'Yes and yes and yes. I married a Frenchman, three children, still working as a translator. Life has been good to me. But tell me about you. You're married I assume?'

'I live alone, but that's okay.'

It was her turn to laugh. 'Sometimes I wish I did, too. Tell me about the home country, Joe. I haven't been back since my parents died. Not in twenty years. I read the papers, sometimes I hear things through embassy channels. Is the situation as bad as ever?'

'Quieter now,' I said. 'No one much left to fight back. It's always quieter when there's no one left to fight, isn't it?'

'Of course,' she said.

'But life goes on.'

'Yes.'

'And it's wonderful to hear your voice again.'

'Thank you. I needed to talk to you.'

'I really do appreciate your calling. And things are okay, you know, they're okay.'

'That's good to hear.'

'And the country will outlive what's been going on. It'll rise again.'

'That's good to hear too.' She paused. 'There's another reason I called. Something else I needed to tell you.'

Outside the workshop window the evening was settling on the empty branches of the winter trees, nesting for the night. It was that time of day when everything is stark against the blank sky and there's a beautiful austerity, made all the more precious by the knowledge that it cannot last.

'There was a baby, Joe. After that summer, after you came to stay that weekend. There was a baby.'

I imagined all the birds along the telephone wires taking sudden flight.

'I lost her after five months.'

I sat down, all my energy gone.

'A girl?' I heard myself ask.

'That's what I felt, that's what I sensed. I would have told you, had she lived. I should have told you, but at the time I was away from home and everything seemed out of control. I can only put my not telling you down to the uncertainty of youth. I apologise.'

'There's no need to apologise. I'm so glad you told me now.'

'Are you?'

'Of course I am. I'm smiling.'

'Really?'

'Yes,' I said, and I was.

Ruth started to say something, but the words jagged in her throat and I heard a sob.

'Life passes quickly,' she said at last. 'And we have no idea about the end of days.'

And then she began to laugh, a nervous laugh.

'Listen to me,' she said, 'getting all philosophical and maudlin. That's not why I called. I called to tell you and to talk to you and to say I hope you're well. Not to change your life or my life, just to tell you about the baby, about our little girl.'

We said some other things; I don't remember them now. I don't think they were of any consequence. I didn't ask Ruth for a number or a contact address, and she didn't offer one. There was no need. We said our good-byes and she was gone.

I sat for a very long time, long past the falling of darkness and the disappearance of the winter branches into the cold night, and a sensation of great warmth, great happiness and optimism flowed through me, and I thought: that's the thing, isn't it, if a man has hope, he has something.